Dear Diary,

I'm worried about Ellie. Oh, not as the administrator of Maitland Maternity. No, what I'm worried about is the rest of her life. Mostly because there isn't one.

Of all my children, Ellie is the one I would have chosen most likely to succeed. Her gifts are so obvious to me. I don't understand why she can't see them for herself.

I know it all goes back to that episode with Sloan Cassidy when she was in high school. Ellie's always taken things so seriously. I'm afraid she took Sloan too seriously. And I did her a terrible disservice. I thought if I didn't make a big deal of the whole thing, she wouldn't either. But I was wrong. I should have helped her through that time. As it stands, I fear that the heart Sloan Cassidy broke has never healed.

But I'm not giving up hope. Especially now. I heard Sloan just came by looking for Ellie. I don't dare hope that Sloan and Ellie can find what Ellie thought they had all those years ago. But if Ellie could see him again, as a mature adult, maybe, just maybe she could get over him and get on with her life. When it comes to Ellie, I care so very much....

Dear Reader,

There's never a dull moment at Maitland Maternity! This unique and now world-renowned clinic was founded twenty-five years ago by Megan Maitland, widow of William Maitland, of the prominent Austin, Texas, Maitlands. Megan is also matriarch of an impressive family of seven children, many of whom are active participants in the everyday miracles that bring children into the world.

As our series begins, the family is stunned by the unexpected arrival of an unidentified baby at the clinic—unidentified, except for the claim that the child is a Maitland. Who are the parents of this child? Is the claim legitimate? Will the media's tenacious grip on this news damage the clinic's reputation? Suddenly, rumors and counterclaims abound. Women claiming to be the child's mother materialize out of the woodwork! How will Megan get at the truth? And how will the media circus affect the lives and loves of the Maitland children—Abby, the head of gynecology, Ellie, the hospital administrator, her twin sister, Beth, who runs the day care center, Mitchell, the fertility specialist, R.J., the vice president of operations— even Anna, who has nothing to do with the clinic, and Jake, the black sheep of the family?

Please join us each month over the next year as the mystery of the Maitland baby unravels, bit by enticing bit, and book by captivating book!

Marsha Zinberg,
Senior Editor and Editorial Co-ordinator, Special Projects

# TARA TAYLOR QUINN

## Cassidy's Kids

Silhouette Books

Published by Silhouette Books
America's Publisher of Contemporary Romance

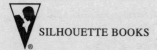

**SILHOUETTE BOOKS**

ISBN-13: 978-0-373-65063-7

CASSIDY'S KIDS

Copyright © 2000 by Harlequin Books S.A.

Tara Taylor Quinn is acknowledged as the author of this work.

Recycling programs for this product may not exist in your area.

Visit Silhouette Books at www.eHarlequin.com

**Printed in U.S.A.**

**Tara Taylor Quinn**'s first book, *Yesterday's Secrets,* was published by Harlequin in October 1993. It received two Reviewers' Choice nominations, and was a finalist for the RWA RITA Award. After nineteen titles in six years, there are over three million copies of Tara's books in print. They have been nominated for several awards, and have appeared on many bestseller lists.

Tara Taylor Quinn's love affair with Harlequin Books began when she was fourteen years old and picked up a free promotional copy of a Harlequin Romance in her hometown grocery store. The relationship was solidified the year she was suspended from her high school typing class for hiding a Harlequin Romance behind the keys of her electric typewriter. Unaware that her instructor loomed close by, Ms. Quinn read blissfully on with one finger resting on the automatically repeating period key. She finished the book in the principal's office.

When she's not writing, fulfilling speaking engagements or performing the many duties required by her position as regional director on the National Board of the Romance Writers of America, Ms. Quinn spends her time with her husband, and commutes to Arizona State University with her fourteen-year-old senior psychology major daughter, Rachel.

For Rachel Marie Reames, the heart and soul of my life;

And
Dana Mariah Bodell, my little soul mate:

Without the two of you, your sweet laughter,
your company and encouragement,
your inspiration and bowls of cottage cheese,
this book would not have happened. Thanks, girls!

# CHAPTER ONE

THE BRIGHT SIDE was that nothing else could go wrong. Everything already had. At breakfast that morning, sitting in the same chair at the same dining room table she'd been sitting at almost since the day she was born, Ellie Maitland had had a panic attack. Out of the blue, she'd suddenly felt suffocated by that sameness, by the inadequacies that had shaped her life and which spelled out an entire future of more of the same. Her hands had started to tingle, and her feet, too, almost as though they'd all fallen asleep at once.

"Hey, El, I saw that you picked up my dry cleaning again—"

Her twin sister's voice seemed to be coming through a megaphone rather than from across the table.

"—you didn't have to do that."

"I knew you'd forgotten, and I had to drive by that way, anyway," Ellie replied. Focusing on something as mundane as the laundry helped a bit. But only until she looked down again.

Staring at the newspaper in front of her, at yet another article subtly hinting that Eleanor Maitland might not be up to her recently appointed position as administrator at Maitland Maternity Clinic, Ellie had to concentrate to keep the words from blurring. She was losing it. Twenty-five years old and falling apart.

"Ignore them, Ellie." The soft feminine voice was

laced with the steely determination that had seen Megan Maitland through her own lifetime of disappointments and joys.

Grasping the business section of the large Texas newspaper between cold fingers, Ellie finally looked up from the hurtful words. "They're like vultures, Mom, waiting for me to fail."

"So?" Megan's dark blue eyes didn't waver as they met the troubled look of her second-youngest-by-eleven—inutes daughter.

"They think I only got this job because I'm your daughter."

"So?"

"Is it true?" Ellie asked, bracing herself.

Beth, her twin, scoffed.

"What do you think?" Megan's expression was shrewd.

"I have goals, Mom. And a clear sense of our mission."

Megan nodded and smiled. "I know."

"No one else would have hired me so young for a position of such stature."

"Probably not."

"And certainly not while I'm still a semester away from my master's degree."

"You're going to night school. You'll have your degree before the fiscal year ends."

Ellie flushed under her mother's loving gaze. No matter how often Ellie fell short of being everything a Maitland should be, Megan continued to love her. "I won't let you down," she whispered, afraid she was really going to make a fool of herself and cry.

Ellie never cried. At least not where anyone in her family could see.

"I know you won't," Megan said.

And that had been that. Ellie, the ugly duckling baby Maitland, might not feel she was an asset to the family, but they were generous enough to love her anyway. And she had just enough Maitland blood running through her veins to make certain that she didn't let them down. At least not professionally.

Which was why, sitting at her desk later that morning, she refused to back down when the man who serviced their current piping system tried to convince her not to invest in a new, upgraded one. Maitland Maternity, the clinic founded by her mother and late father almost twenty-five years ago, had outgrown its present system, and Ellie would not put the clinic's patients—or reputation—at risk.

Once the man had left, she turned back to the financial statements Drake Logan, Maitland's VP of finance, had left her.

"Ellie—?"

At the sound of the voice she froze. She'd been wrong. Things could get worse.

"—I'm sorry to barge in, but the phone just seemed so cold after all this time."

Heart pounding, Ellie stared at the handsome man standing in her doorway. He wasn't supposed to just show up at her office. He wasn't supposed to show up at all. She'd gotten over him years ago. Wasn't ever going to have to see him again.

"I can't believe you're here." It was the only thought she had.

Forcing herself, she rose, offered her hand, pretended that warm touch of his calloused fingers did nothing to her.

The only plausible reason she could come up with for

his sudden appearance was that he and his wife, Marla, needed the clinic's services.

"You look great!" he said, admiration in his voice and in the steady brown gaze that was taking in every inch of her.

"So do you." Gorgeous. Incredible. And in her office. Damn him.

"You're the boss now, huh?" he asked. He looked around her big office, but only briefly, then his eyes focused back on her.

Nodding, Ellie started to sweat. Seeing him after all this time couldn't mean anything to her. *He* couldn't mean anything to her.

"I knew you'd make it to the top quicker than anyone," he said, his voice full of easy camaraderie.

"Why are you here?" she blurted, feeling the need to get rid of him before she made a fool of herself and hugged him or something. Maybe he'd forgotten their last, devastating conversation, but she hadn't. It had shaped every day of her life since.

"I need a favor."

His voice was sexier than she remembered it. Deeper. "What's it been, ten years?" she asked, trying to smile in spite of the tension. He actually thought that he could waltz in after all this time, and she'd be waiting to do his bidding.

Not that she could blame him completely. Practically every girl in their high school—Ellie included—had done just that. Sloan was definitely one of God's gifts to the world's female population, though one with a cruel twist when it had come to Ellie.

"'Bout that," he said. He didn't appear to be the least bit contrite about the ten year lapse, though age seemed to have taken the edge off his supreme self-confidence. "I've wanted to stop in many times, Ellie, to see you."

"So why didn't you?"

"I figured it was best just to leave well enough alone."

Which was just about the best non-answer she'd ever heard.

"Until now," she reminded him.

He shrugged. "I'm in trouble, and you're the only one I know of who can help."

She wasn't going to be party to his and Marla's family problems. No matter how nicely he asked.

Leaning forward, resting her thighs against her desk, Ellie crossed her arms over her chest. "So how've you been?" she asked, and then made herself continue, "How's Marla?"

"I wouldn't know." He didn't take his eyes off her. "She's in New York."

She hadn't heard about that. But then, lately she'd been concerned about the problems in her own family.

"What's she doing in New York?" *Is she still your wife?*

"Trying to act, last I heard." His eyes continued to assess her. "We were divorced six months ago."

Ellie sat down. Hard. Sloan was divorced. No one had told her.

"Y-you said you had a favor to ask."

Divorced, he was more dangerous than ever. She had to get rid of him. To focus on what mattered. Her goals. The clinic. Getting through the day.

"I know it's presumptuous, me coming in here like this after all this time, but I'm at my wits' end, Ellie, and I don't know where else to turn. We were pretty special friends once."

Opening her mouth to grant him whatever he asked, Ellie bit her tongue, instead. She was working day and night trying to prove herself—and going to night school besides. She didn't have time to spare for him. Or to risk another broken heart. Sloan Cassidy had had his chance.

"I'd never ask for myself—" Sloan's big brown eyes were imploring her, and his body made an imposing figure in skin-tight, earth-worn denim and a corduroy shirt that fit his cowboy bulkiness to perfection.

"But the girls are getting so out of hand that if I don't do something soon, it may be too late."

*The girls?* Ellie swallowed, glad she'd bitten her tongue. Even after ten years, hearing about Sloan's relations with the opposite sex still hurt. There'd never been just one girl in love with him, panting after him: there'd never been fewer than a dozen.

"What, exactly, is it you want from me?" She was curious, that was all. And maybe a bit of a masochist. Entertaining visions of herself posing as Sloan's fiancée long enough to ward off the troublesome women, Ellie almost smiled again.

"Just some pointers, Ellie. Teach me how to raise them."

"Raise them?"

"You know how I grew up, El. My own folks didn't set such a hot example. I'd already been having trouble getting the dad stuff down right. I'm a complete failure at the mom part."

*Mom? Dad?* Feeling a resurgence of the panic attack from earlier that morning, Ellie forced her fingers to relax their grip on the arms of her chair. "Just how old are they?" she asked. Sloan was a father? More than once? Somehow she'd just never pictured homecoming-queen, cheerleader-captain Marla having babies. Not even for Sloan.

"Eighteen months." He looked desperate, standing there in front of her. Desperate and needy. Which was the only reason Ellie didn't have him removed from her office.

"And?" He'd said *girls,* plural.

"That's it. I have eighteen—onth-old twin daughters who are holy terrors, and not particularly happy, either."

The catch Ellie felt in her chest must be part of the panic attack she was fighting. It had absolutely nothing to do with the mention of *Sloan* and *daughters* in the same sentence. There was no reason why she should feel a longing at the mention that they were twins. Or a kinship, either.

"I have no idea what to do for them."

Ellie didn't do kids. Period. They weren't in her five-year plan. She had to stay focused. To keep her mind on the things she could have, and off the things she couldn't. To control what little about her life she *could* control.

"What makes you think I could help?" she asked as if from outside herself—morbidly curious, she supposed.

Sloan's gesture encompassed her office and the clinic outside her door. "You're in the baby business."

"Wrong." She shook her head. "I'm in the administration business." She left the baby part of the Maitland family business to those who were qualified.

His eyes narrowed as he watched her fiddle with a mechanical pencil on top of her desk. "You're a twin." The words were softly spoken.

And Sloan knew how hard that had been for her, Ellie

thought. Growing up in the shadow of her beautiful, vivacious sister. She shrugged. "Doesn't make me an expert on raising children."

Placing both hands on her desk, Sloan leaned forward until his eyes were almost level with hers. She could smell the musky scent of his aftershave, mixed with leather and outdoors and all that was Sloan. "Please, Ellie, at least think about it?"

This had to stop. "I can't, Sloan."

"Just think about it," he said again, straightening. "At least meet them, then see how you feel."

"No!" She stood, smoothing the skirt of her practical business suit, forcing herself to calm down. "I really don't have time right now to take on another project, Sloan." She spoke with every ounce of authority she possessed. And hoped it was enough.

Ellie wasn't as relieved as she might have been when, without another word, Sloan nodded, turned and left. His last discerning glance haunted her for the rest of the afternoon, and she had an awful feeling he would be back.

THOSE DAMN INCREDIBLY blue eyes tormented Sloan as he turned his pickup truck away from Austin toward the open road and the relative safety of his ranch. Ellie's eyes were still as filled with determination as they'd been when he'd known her ten years ago. Still emanating an intelligence that was intimidating, or challenging, depending on how you chose to look at it. Sloan, fool that he was, had always been more prone to rising to a challenge than wisely giving in to intimidation.

Ellie—still as sexy as ever.

All they'd ever been was friends. Great friends. On

his side, best friends. Ellie had never known how he'd lusted after her. He'd made certain she'd never known.

Swerving so hard his tires shot gravel up past the roof of the truck, Sloan came to a sudden stop in the parking lot of a tavern he hadn't visited in years. Ariel and Alisha were safe with Charlie's sister for the afternoon. Their father needed a drink.

Too bad his housekeeper's sister had to go back home to Arizona at the end of the week. Too bad she was already married and seventy years old.

Up at the bar a few minutes later, a cold mug of beer clasped in his fist, Sloan amended that last thought about Charlie's sister, Mary. Too bad she was *married*. Seventy years old wasn't a problem.

Right. And maybe cow manure could fly.


*WHY DIDN'T THE CRYING STOP?*

Rolling over groggily, raising a hand to push the cropped strands of dark hair out of her face, Ellie groaned. The family mansion was just too small for both her and the mystery baby. Only two months old, he still wasn't sleeping through the night.

Consequently, neither was Ellie.

It was hard to get used to having a baby in the house, but the tiny boy had been abandoned on the steps of the clinic with a note claiming he was a Maitland, too, and Megan's heart had gone out to the infant. She'd been made his foster mother until the child's real parents were found.

Ellie winced. Her brothers had become prime suspects as the baby's father, though she couldn't make herself believe any of them had really created the disruptive human being down the hall.

She rolled over again and tried to ignore the baby's

cries, but they grew louder, more urgent. And it suddenly dawned on Ellie why that was.

She was in charge.

Amy, the nurse her mother had hired to care for the baby, was out of town for a couple of days for a family emergency. And Beth and Megan were out, probably until dawn, at a high-profile fund-raiser Ellie had begged not to attend. With all of the negative publicity Maitland Maternity had suffered through in the past month, it was imperative that the family be represented. But not by Ellie. She was still under close scrutiny after her appointment as the clinic's administrator, and with her lack of sophisticated wit, and no typical Maitland knock 'em dead looks to make up for the lack, she'd been afraid of doing more harm than good. Or at least, that had been her excuse. She'd really just wanted a quiet night at home to regroup after the day she'd had.

Ellie dragged herself out of bed and slogged down the hall to the nursery Megan had set up in the wing Beth and Ellie shared at Maitland Mansion. "I'm coming," she called to the hostile baby, picking up her pace a bit. After all, it wasn't the little guy's fault he'd had such rotten luck in life.

Unless, of course, he'd carried on this way right from the start and his poor mother had been as hopeless as Ellie in knowing how to quiet him.

"Shh, Cody," she demanded as she entered the nursery, the air warm on legs left bare by her cotton shorts and matching short sleeved pajama top. Heart picking up speed as she looked at the beet-red face of the baby, she softened her voice. "Hey, little man, what's up?"

With arms trembling—from lack of sleep, she told herself—Ellie reached down to scoop up the hot bundle.

He wasn't only hot, he was soaked. And not just from sweat and tears, though there was plenty of both.

The initial bout of crying stopped the moment Ellie picked Cody up out of his crib. His tear-drenched eyelashes blinked as he stared up at her. As well he should. He'd have no idea who this stranger holding him might be.

In spite of his soggy state, Ellie stopped and stared right back at the miniature Maitland. She'd never been this close to him before.

From the moment he'd shown up on the doorstep of the clinic, and Megan had announced she would be taking temporary custody of him, Ellie had entered a new goal in the log book in her mind. She wasn't going to hold him the way her sister Beth kept doing. She couldn't. Ellie was much more intense than Beth. She'd never learned to live for the moment the way her more outgoing sister had done since birth. And it made no sense to grow attached to a child who was in their home only temporarily.

There was no point in torturing herself with something she knew she would never have. Which was also why she never visited the nursery at the clinic unless she was there on official business. She'd learned a long time ago that the way to be happy—or at least successful—was to avoid distractions.

It went without saying that in Ellie's book a virgin with no prospects at the age of twenty-five would likely never have a baby.

Ellie stared, frozen. The baby's warmth seeped through her pajamas, along with other things, until his little face screwed up with displeasure once again. "Okay, hold on," she said urgently as she rushed him over to his new change table. "I'm fairly certain I can figure out how to change a diaper."

Actually, she knew she could. She'd changed hundreds of them during her teens when she'd filled her dateless nights with baby-sitting jobs and dreams of having babies of her own. Babies that would love her in spite of her quiet personality and drab looks.

Amazingly enough, her voice seemed to have a calming effect on baby Cody. As long as she was speaking, his howls stopped, and he stared up at her. Ellie kept up a stream of senseless chatter while she went to work on the baby's wet diaper.

"I don't know which one of my brothers—or cousins, for that matter—is responsible for you, little man, but I can promise you that we'll find out eventually, and when we do, I'm going to choke the life out of him with my bare hands."

The wet sleeper and diaper came off effortlessly. Ellie reconsidered what she'd just said in lieu of the baby's sensibilities and the frown on his scrunched up little face.

"Okay, we'll let him live, but only because you need a daddy to teach you how to play baseball," she amended. "But I get to at least yell at him first, okay?"

Cody's legs flailed as Ellie cleaned and powdered him before expertly applying a dry diaper and sleeper.

There were bottles of formula already made up in the refrigerator in one corner of the nursery, and a bottle warmer on the counter beside it. With the baby lodged in one arm, Ellie used her free hand to prepare Cody's late-night meal.

She hated to think of one of her beloved older brothers being guilty of fathering this abandoned child. Which was maybe another reason why she'd refused to acknowledge the baby's presence in their lives as little more than an administrator's public relations problem.

"The truth is, little guy, that when I think about it, almost any one of them *could* be responsible."

After testing the warming formula on the inside of her wrist, Ellie settled into the rocker her mother had had brought down from the attic. Until that night, Ellie had been hoping Cody wasn't really a Maitland at all, but rather a scam on the part of some sick woman to tap into the Maitland fortune.

But holding the baby close to her breast, taking in features that were distinctive even at such a young age, she knew in her heart what Megan must have known from the minute she'd first unwrapped him in the doorway of Maitland Maternity a month ago. Cody could very well be a Maitland.

Sucking greedily, the baby ate, innocently unaware of the commotion his existence was causing in the lives of so many people. Ellie had only thought about the damage the baby's sudden appearance was doing to the Maitland family and, by extension, the clinic. Now, as her heart and body warmed at the noisy sounds of the baby eating, as his little fist came to rest intimately against her breast, she couldn't help but think about the damage that could be done to this innocent little child.

Was he to live with the stigma of his abandonment for his entire life? Was it going to remain like a dead weight, creating feelings of unworthiness that would follow him into adulthood?

Getting angrier, and more possessive, by the moment, Ellie gently burped Cody and rocked him long after he'd fallen asleep in her arms. Who, in her right mind, could hold this precious bundle in her arms and then abandon him? How could one of her relatives have slept so irresponsibly with such a woman?

And who was the baby's father? R.J.? As Maitland Maternity's president, he'd certainly have reasons not to come forward if he were responsible. But would his personal integrity allow him to stay silent? Of course not.

And what about Mitch? Ellie couldn't believe he'd lied when he'd so sheepishly admitted that he hadn't been with a woman in over a year. He was a fertility specialist. He'd know that eventually the baby's paternity could be proven, once their mother approved the testing. He'd know it was useless not to come forward. Unless he'd donated some of his own sperm to his experimental bank and didn't know it had been used...

Then there was Jake. A tear splashed against the sleeping baby's face, and Ellie started guiltily, wiping the wet drop away. Jake was the most likely suspect of her three brothers. And the one she least wanted it to be. She adored all of her brothers, but Jake was special. He was different. He was her hero. He'd never have fathered this helpless child without knowing it. And he'd never have allowed the baby to be abandoned. No matter what lines Jake crossed in his life, he'd never cross that one.

Ellie rocked the baby until her muscles were cramped. An hour passed, then two, and still she wasn't ready to give up her burden. It was a night out of time. A secret night, when Ellie could be Ellie, and no one would ever know; a night that would never ask questions.

Finally, when she was afraid her tears would wake the baby again, she laid him gently in his crib, covered his diaper plump rear with a light blanket and tiptoed back to her room. She'd hoped the stark familiarity of her room would shock her back to normalcy. Wiping the tears away, she wanted to pretend that they'd never fallen. That the tiny body in the other room hadn't opened up a door she'd thought rusted shut years before.

Changing her stained pajamas for a clean pair, she climbed between her sheets, trying to soothe herself back to sleep using numbers, the way she'd been doing for most of her life. She started with smaller figures, afraid her concentration would be overstimulated by the larger ones she more commonly used these days. But even the smaller ones wouldn't line up. They danced around on the stage in her mind. Changing colors. And form. Trying to escape, to get away from her before she could force them into their logical places.

And as she struggled, tossing and turning in her attempt to control the images in her head, the numbers were replaced by Sloan's face. By two imaginary little female versions of his face. One plus two equals three. With baby Cody's heat still warming her body, she couldn't stop the images, couldn't help wondering if Sloan's baby girls would feel just as wonderful, just as right, up against her.

Then onto the scene came a fourth image. Three plus one, after all, always equaled four. Marla. The mother of Sloan's children. The beautiful woman Sloan had never stopped dating during the entire time he'd known Ellie. The woman he'd been out with after he'd kissed Ellie so passionately.

She'd be a fool to open herself up to that kind of pain again. And Ellie Maitland was no fool.

# CHAPTER TWO

SLOAN HID OUT in the barn the next morning. Mary had come to work with Charlie again, wanting, she claimed, to spend as much time with her brother as she could before leaving. But instead of staying in the house with Charlie, she was watching Sloan's girls. Sloan half wondered if maybe the woman wasn't trying to figure out a way to take his daughters home with her.

Damn thing was, the way the girls responded to her, he wasn't sure that wasn't what they'd want, too, if they'd been old enough to have a say in the matter.

From his position inside Ronnie's stall, he could hear them outside in the yard, giggling as they chased a butterfly. He stopped mucking long enough to peek out the door of the barn. Smiling, he watched his daughters play. Sloan was itching to join them, but forced himself to return to his mare's stall, instead. If he gave in to his desire, if he went out into the yard, the happy little imps tumbling over their feet and laughing so delightfully would turn into demanding, whiny little patoots.

"You've got time to waste mucking out a clean stall?"

Sloan turned when he heard Charlie's voice. The old man had been with Sloan since before he'd married Marla. Charlie'd lost a leg riding the rodeo circuit and had been wandering around the circuit drunk all the time, making what money he could as a bookie, when

Sloan first hit the scene. But in spite of his own problems, Charlie had taken the teenaged Sloan under his
wing, become a crotchety but caring father figure, and
had coached Sloan all the way to the top. And when
Sloan had made enough money to turn his parents'
dilapidated excuse for Texas farmland into the four-
thousand acre growing cattle concern it was now, Charlie had gladly turned in his bottle and betting tallies for
a dishrag and washing machine. Lucky for Sloan, the old
man had turned out to be a halfway decent cook, too.

"Not really," Sloan finally said, resuming the work
he'd begun after checking the cattle's salt and mineral
supplements that morning. Though he hired part-tim-
ers to help with vaccinating and shipping calves, Sloan
usually worked the ranch alone.

Charlie watched silently for a couple more minutes,
and Sloan waited. Charlie must have something more
on his mind than Sloan's chores, to have made the trek
out to the barn in the first place.

"Mary's got the name of a woman who can come
in every day during the week to watch those mites for
ya."

The old man could have saved himself the trip out if
that's what he'd come to say. "Thanks."

"I'll give her a call if you like—get her out here to
meet with ya."

"Not necessary, thanks."

Charlie leaned against the edge of the stall. "You
can't do this all alone, Sloan, no matter how bad you
want to."

"I know."

"So you'll call this woman?"

"I don't want my girls raised by a baby-sitter." Sloan,
wishing that Ronnie weren't such a fastidious horse, that

she made more of a mess, cleared the last of what little debris there was from the stall. "I may not be much in the way of parenting material, but I'm going to learn," he said. "I can't do anything about Marla's abandonment, but I can damn well make certain that those babies don't feel unwanted."

"But you—"

"I mean it, Charlie," Sloan interrupted, leaning on his pitchfork as he met the other man's gaze. "I know what it feels like to be deserted, not just by a parent who left, but worse, by one who didn't, who lived in the same house but just wasn't there. My children will not suffer the same insecurities I had to work through."

"Not to mention the loneliness," Charlie said gruffly.

Sloan grunted and attacked the fresh bale of hay he intended to spread on the floor of Ronnie's stall. Charlie knew far too much.

"That's why you married Marla, wasn't it? To get away from the loneliness?"

"I married her for the sex."

Charlie nodded. "I figured it wasn't for love."

Stopping again, Sloan frowned. "I cared about Marla."

"So much so that when she was fooling around with the jerks in town, you barely missed a beat."

He could hardly hate his wife for infidelity when the same urge was something he fought every day of his life. He'd been stubborn enough to win the battle, blessed, apparently, with incredible self-control, but he could still empathize with his wife's weakness. Sloan—the man who wanted every woman who'd ever been born.

"She was sorry. She stopped."

"If you'd been in love with her, you'd have wanted to kill the guys."

"I'm not the violent type."

Charlie's weather-worn face showed no expression. Unless, thought Sloan, you looked into the deep gray eyes that saw far more than they should.

"I didn't notice you sheddin' any tears when she finally left town."

"I never stopped trying to make it work," Sloan protested.

"But did you ever love her?"

"I worked at it every day of our marriage."

"You can't force love to happen."

"What's your point, old man?" Sloan asked, getting impatient. "Don't you have some dishes to wash or something?"

"Point is," Charlie said, straightening, his prosthesis not even noticeable as he walked toward the barn door, "you couldn't force yourself to love Marla no matter what you'd made up your mind to do, and you can't force them girlies to be happy, either."

"I love them. That should be enough."

"You spoil them."

"I love them," Sloan said firmly.

"You let them run you around worse than that self-centered bitch you married."

"I love them." Sloan wasn't backing down. He was used to Charlie's bluntness.

"Then figure out how to do it right, or hire someone to come do it for you," Charlie shot back. "Those babes are hell to live with when you're around."

His housekeeper's parting words stung.

NOT WANTING A REPEAT of the morning before, Ellie skipped breakfast at home and went in to work early. It was just lucky coincidence that by missing breakfast, she also managed to avoid her family members—and baby Cody—as well. She hadn't slept well. Was cranky and out of sorts. She needed to immerse herself in her work, remind herself what mattered in her life. As uptight and serious as she was, her career was all she was going to have, and she was damn well going to be happy about that.

But by ten o'clock that morning, she was also starving. Breakfast was the most important meal of the day, and she'd robbed herself of that sustenance. She was falling asleep at her desk. A tall glass of diet cola and one of Joe's four-cheese western omelettes were definitely in order.

A dose of Mary Jane's sweetness wouldn't be amiss, either. Grabbing the Asleep at the Wheel CD she'd found for her country-western-fanatic friend, Ellie checked out with Megan and took a much-needed break.

Austin Eats Diner, located right next door to the clinic on the corner of prestigious Mayfair Avenue and Hill Drive, was just the diversion Ellie needed. Mary Jane Potter who was waiting on a group of cowboys at the counter, looked up and waved as Ellie walked in. Feeling better already, Ellie smiled, waved back and seated herself at a table for two. Though Mary Jane was three years younger than Ellie, she was one of Ellie's closest friends. The petite brunette had grown up next door to Lana Lord, Ellie and Beth's other best friend, and the four had seen each other through all the crises of adolescence.

Watching Mary Jane keep everyone in the bustling diner happy, Ellie relaxed for the first time since she'd seen Sloan Cassidy the day before. She hadn't told anyone about Sloan's unexpected visit. Nor was she certain she was going to. But she wasn't going to deny herself the comfort of drawing silent strength from her friends.

"You skipped breakfast again?" Mary Jane asked, bringing Ellie the diet cola she hadn't yet asked for.

"I had some work to catch up on," Ellie said, meeting the smile in Mary Jane's eyes.

Mary Jane's gaze turned to concern. "You're going to work yourself to death, Ellie, and it's just not worth it."

Taking in the mostly full tables around her, Ellie chose to ignore her friend's warning. Mary Jane just didn't understand. No one did. "I've only been in the position six months," she defended herself. "There's always a lot of extra time invested in a new job."

"Fourteen hours a day?" Mary Jane scoffed, seemingly unaware of the thirty other patrons sitting in the brightly colored restaurant. "You haven't been out with Lana and Beth and me in months."

"School started," Ellie responded. "I've got classes at night."

"One night a week."

"Hey, what is this?" Ellie started to get annoyed, but only because she so desperately needed Mary Jane's support. "I come here to eat and get yelled at?"

Mary Jane sighed. "I'm not yelling, El. I just care."

"I know." That was the sustenance she'd really been after. "Things'll calm down soon, I promise."

Mary Jane nodded but didn't look any happier; she pulled her pad and pen out of her pocket. "You want the omelette?"

"Yes, please." Ellie picked up the CD from the seat beside her. "I brought you this."

"'Let's Ride With Bob' by Asleep at the Wheel?" Mary Jane's eyes lit up. "Where'd you find it?"

"A record shop downtown. I needed some more George Winston."

Reaching into her pocket, Mary Jane asked, "What do I owe you?"

"Nothing," Ellie replied, brushing it off. "Just don't make me listen to any more of Bob Will's Texas swing band stuff. I prefer horns to fiddles and steel guitars."

"Thanks, El—"

Mary Jane smiled warmly again, and Ellie got all the payment she needed.

"I can't believe you remembered I wanted this. You're the best."

Embarrassed, Ellie shook her head. "What I am is hungry."

Mary Jane grinned. "Be right back." And then she was off, pouring coffee, delivering heavy plates of food, spreading her cheery smile all over the room. Sitting back, watching her friend, Ellie counted her blessings.

She was taking the last bite of an incredibly delicious omelette when Shelby Lord, the diner's owner and Lana's triplet sister, suddenly appeared from the back room with a young blond woman at her side. Spotting Ellie, Shelby made a beeline for her table, stranger in tow.

"Ellie! I'm glad you're here," Shelby said. "I want you to meet Sara. She's going to be waitressing here starting this afternoon."

The blonde looked to be about Ellie's age, but there didn't seem to be twenty-five years of life lurking in her blue eyes. Rather, her gaze appeared almost vacant, though intelligent. If such a contrast were possible.

Shelby put a supportive arm around Sara's back, drawing her forward.

"Sara's suffering from amnesia," Shelby said softly. Motioning for Sara to take the chair across from Ellie, Shelby pulled up a third chair for herself.

"I don't think it's necessary for everyone to know," she continued, "but I thought you should."

Instantly filled with compassion, Ellie took in the other woman's soft features. "You don't remember anything?" she asked. She couldn't imagine something so horrible. To have no control at all.

Sara shook her head. "A policeman found me in an alley, and I had no idea how I came to be there. He took me to a women's shelter."

"How frightening."

Sara smiled sadly. "It was. I remember waking up, but I had no idea where I was. I only know that it was really dark. And my head hurt."

Horrified, Ellie leaned forward. "You'd been attacked?"

"We don't know." Sara shrugged nonchalantly, but her eyes told a different story. Filled with fear, they testified to the seriousness of her predicament. "The shelter sent me to a free clinic to get checked over, and they couldn't find anything wrong, other than the bump on my head. It had been bleeding, and I had a bit of a concussion, but nothing serious."

"And they couldn't tell how that bump came to be there?" Ellie was a stickler for details. She was never satisfied until she had all the answers. And this woman, with her sweet smile, looked like she *deserved* some answers.

"I could have been attacked, I suppose, but it's just as likely that I fell, or that something fell on me."

"She had nothing on her when she wandered into the shelter," Shelby added. "No purse, no jewelry, nothing."

Experiencing the woman's pain almost as though it were her own, Ellie couldn't let go. "So what are you going to do?"

"Work here, be patient, hope my memory comes back soon." Sara's tone implied there was little else she could do.

"Did you check, the missing persons' reports?"

"Yeah," Sara's eyes clouded. "Apparently no one has reported me missing, at least not in Austin."

"What about the papers?" Ellie asked.

"The police have no way of knowing how far back to check," Shelby said, reaching over to give Sara's hand a quick squeeze. "They've gone back a couple of weeks from the time of her appearance, and found nothing."

As she sat there, Ellie put herself in Sara's shoes. And suddenly the problems she'd been having with the press seemed almost a blessing. At least she had a life to report about.

"Where are you going to stay?" Ellie asked, as Mary Jane dropped off another diet cola and was gone.

"Mrs. Parker's Inn," Sara replied, her features more relaxed. "I've already seen the room—it's quite nice, actually, and the house is cozy. I just needed to make certain I had a job before I moved in."

Ellie was familiar with the boarding house. It was comfortable and within walking distance of the diner.

"Speaking of which, we better let you go get settled in so you can be back this afternoon," Shelby said, standing.

Sara scrambled to her feet, as well, including both Ellie and Shelby with her genuine smile. "I'll see you later, then. Nice to meet you, Ellie." And she was gone.

As Ellie walked back to the clinic and the mounds of work waiting for her there, she couldn't get Sara out of her mind or her heart. In losing her memory, Sara had in essence lost her life, lost everything that mattered.

After the previous night with Cody, Ellie couldn't help wondering if she'd lost touch with things that mattered in her life, as well.

*Except my goals,* she reminded herself as she applied herself to the day's work. She would be the best damn administrator Maitland Maternity had ever seen. Her goals might have changed through the years, but having them had always sustained her. They'd given her a reason to get up in the morning, led her to every success she'd ever had. She couldn't forget that.

JANELLE MAITLAND WAS NOT a patient woman. And she'd been waiting every day for thirty years to claim what was hers. Looking in the cracked mirror of the seedy hotel room in this nameless little dirt-hole Texas town, she felt the unwelcome pressure of frustrated tears behind her eyes. She was a pretty woman, she thought. Her long dark hair and brown eyes screamed privilege. It wasn't right that she had to suffer for her father's weaknesses. She wasn't the one who'd decided to leave the family clan, to squander her life and her share of the family fortune in Las Vegas. She'd had no choice in the way he'd forced her to grow up.

But she wasn't a kid anymore. Her father was dead, which had turned out to be a really good thing. She had choices now, and she was damn well tired of waiting to exercise them. Why did everything have to take so long? She'd been waiting for Petey to get back from his make-over at the hairdresser's for over an hour. She was hungry. She wanted lunch.

And not some damn take-out lunch, either. She was a Maitland. She deserved better.

ELLIE HEARD THE COMMOTION in the hallway before she actually saw them. She'd been poring over needle codes and standards, planning to upgrade the kind they'd been using at the clinic for more than ten years, when the first shrill "No!" reached her ears. Followed quickly by a babyish "Da-ee! Up!"

Before she could go to investigate, the sounds came closer, and three bodies materialized in her doorway. Sloan, carrying two of the loveliest baby girls she'd ever seen. Or attempting to carry them. Baby girl on the right apparently didn't want to share her daddy's arms and was attempting to push baby girl on the left back down to the floor.

"No!" the baby on the right screamed again. "Isha, down."

To which the toddler on the left let fly with her rendition of "Up! Da-ee, up!"

"Ariel, Alisha, stop this instant." Sloan's voice could have carried a bit more conviction. He smiled apologetically at Ellie before taking a seat in front of her desk and settling the twins, still squabbling, one on each knee.

"Can I help you?" Ellie said, dumbstruck. What in hell was he doing here?

At the sound of her voice, the girls stopped fussing and stared.

"I wanted you to meet them," Sloan said simply. "These are my daughters. Ariel—" he nodded to the baby on the right "—and Alisha. Alisha has the little swirled tuft in the middle of her hairline. I couldn't have ordered up a better way to tell them apart."

When Ellie looked at Ariel, she buried her face in Sloan's chest. Alisha continued to stare, a leftover tear trembling on her lashes.

Ellie fell in love.

"They're beautiful," she said, forgetting that she wanted this man out of her life forever.

"They take after Marla."

The prick of pain wasn't overwhelming, as pain went, but it shocked Ellie back into the present in a hurry. The girls did take after their blond, beauty-queen mother. And Sloan had taken off after her, too. He'd asked Marla to his senior prom only a week after he'd introduced Ellie to the mysteries of making out.

"I really need your help, El." Sloan's eyes beseeched her.

"No." She couldn't. She wasn't that strong. "I have no time as it is," she said lamely. "I'm still getting settled in here. I'm going to school for my MBA. I haven't even been out with my friends in weeks."

No matter how compelling the argument sounded to Ellie, Sloan didn't look convinced.

"Sounds familiar," he said, smiling instead. "As I recall, you were in a similar predicament your sophomore year in high school."

The year she'd met Sloan.

"You didn't want to help with the homecoming float because you were in all the honor classes and were studying for early entrance into college, too. You hadn't been to any of the parties with Beth since the beginning of the school year."

And he'd talked her into helping with the float. It had

been the start of the most wonderful—and most painful—time of her life. She'd felt valuable as a person, and as a woman, for the first time ever. In the end, though, she'd had her insecurities about her sexuality humiliatingly confirmed when Sloan had given her her first kiss and then told her the very next day that they couldn't be friends anymore. He hadn't even waited for the steam to clear before he'd asked Marla to the prom.

"You thanked me for showing you that there was more to life than books, Ellie."

And he'd rewarded her gratitude with heartache. "I can't help you, Sloan." The babies were squirming, but she refused to look at them. She had to get rid of them before she turned traitor on herself, on all she'd learned, on all she'd painstakingly accepted about herself.

A picture of Sara's lost gaze sprang to mind, but Ellie pushed it frantically away. Finding oneself, having meaning in one's life did *not* mean being a fool.

"I don't know how to handle them, Ellie," he said, his gaze so compelling that she couldn't look away. "They're angels until I'm around, and then they transform into little she-devils. They don't mind me. They don't do what I tell them to do."

She couldn't help herself. She looked at the toddlers still perched, albeit precariously, on their father's lap. Perfect little Ariel, and Alisha with her tiny curled cowlick. She saw Beth—and herself. The desire to hold them, to be a part of that private family unit, was so strong that it scared her to death.

"You walked out on me ten years ago, Sloan," she said. *Keep your mind on the things you can have. And off the things you can't have.* "You have no right to come back now just because you don't know how to live with the consequences of your actions."

"It was my senior year, Ellie—I knew I was going to be busy." He stood, one baby on each hip. The girls, as though sensing the tension in the room, sat silently, their little faces turned toward their father. "And I know I don't have the right to ask for your help. But this isn't for me," he continued. "It's for them."

Looking down at his daughters, Sloan swallowed. "You're a twin, Ellie. You work with babies every day. You're smart. And you were always able to see inside me. To help me see."

He wasn't being fair. Ellie swallowed, too, needing to run. She felt another panic attack coming on. Two in two days.

"You wouldn't just come in and do what needed to be done, Ellie. You'd enable me to do it myself." He was still holding her gaze, reaching inside her to the young girl only he'd ever known existed.

"No." She stood, backed up. She just had to find the strength to turn away, then the interview would be over.

"I need you."

She shook her head.

"They need you."

As if on cue, both girls looked up curiously at Ellie. She started to shake; her hands and feet were tingling. She had to make him go.

"Those children are not my responsibility, Sloan. I can't help you."

Ellie's relief when Sloan finally walked away lasted only long enough for her to recognize the woman lurking outside her open office door. *Tattle Today TV* reporter Chelsea Markum had heard every word.

Her stomach knotted painfully, and Ellie wondered

just how big a price she was going to pay for sending Sloan away.

   She wished it were only the television reporter she cared about.

# CHAPTER THREE

"GOT A MINUTE?"

Ellie didn't even bother looking up. "Go away, Chelsea."

"Who was that man who just left here looking like his mother had died?" the reported asked, plopping down in the seat Sloan had just vacated.

"No one."

"You sounded pretty upset for talking to no one," Chelsea said.

Glancing up from the needle codes she was trying desperately to concentrate on, Ellie stared at the auburn-haired reporter. Only a year or two older than herself, Chelsea had the eyes of an old woman. A green-eyed avaricious old woman. And unfortunately they were pinned on Ellie.

"When are you going to give up and go away?" Ellie asked, too weary to deal with the Chelseas of the world today. The woman had been hounding the clinic since baby Cody had made his debut. And when she couldn't get fresh leads on the baby, she turned her roving eye on Ellie, looking for a way to prove the charges of nepotism.

"Sounded like there might be some more abandonment going on."

Chelsea would stop at nothing, it seemed, to get a story. To validate her existence, Ellie thought nastily.

"Not by anyone here," Ellie hated herself for rising to Chelsea's bait. "If you want their story, you'll have to go see their mother in New York."

"Still, it did sound as though you knew the man rather well, and that he wanted something from you."

Ellie bit her tongue.

"That's got to be the most gorgeous man ever to step foot in *your* office," Chelsea baited her, refusing to give up.

"He's a friend from high school," Ellie said, exasperated. "Period."

Crossing one shapely leg over the other, Chelsea nodded, letting the subject drop. "Heard from any of your brothers lately?" she asked.

"I see two of them right here every day," Ellie replied, relaxing a bit as Chelsea reverted to the cat-and—ouse game the two of them had been playing for the past month.

"What about the third—Jake, isn't it?"

Ellie smiled. "Haven't heard from him."

Chelsea sat forward, elbows on her knees. "So who do *you* think fathered that poor baby?" she asked, eyes intent.

If the reporter hadn't had her teeth sunk so fiercely into Ellie, Ellie would almost have admired her. Chelsea was intelligent. Beautiful. And tenacious. She didn't give up. Ellie liked that in a person.

But her teeth were snapping at Ellie—and at the helpless, innocent child Ellie had spent half the night holding. Suddenly the game had changed. The rules were different. It wasn't just the clinic's reputation, the family's reputation that was at stake.

"You stay away from that baby, Chelsea Markum.

He's an innocent child whose life you could permanently affect by your purely fictional innuendoes."

Blinking in surprise, Chelsea sat back, then stood up. "I'm just looking for the truth, Ellie. I have no desire to hurt the kid."

"Right." Ellie stood, too, signaling an end to the unwanted meeting. "Stay out of our lives, Chelsea."

"I'm not the one who chose to live such a public life, Ms. Ellie Administrator Maitland. Maybe you better think about that one."

The reporter's last shot hit Ellie in a sore spot she'd been nursing since she was a child. It had been one of the biggest ironies of her life to be born into the socially prominent Maitland clan. She'd never had the chance to just be the plain Jane she really was. From the moment she was born, she'd had the family reputation to live up to. And it hadn't taken the young Ellie long to figure out that, for her, that was an impossible task.

Her own goals were another story. They were something she could—and did—live up to. Something she could count on. Her goals were realistic, and meeting them brought her peace, if nothing else.

ELLIE WAS JUST PACKING UP for the day, earlier than usual since this was her night at the university, when she had another visitor. A welcome one.

"You in a hurry?" her older sister Abby asked, leaning against the door frame of Ellie's office.

"A little," Ellie told her, but she'd take time, anyway. She could always be a minute or two late for the economics class. She'd read a couple of chapters ahead, anyway.

"Was that Sloan Cassidy I saw leaving earlier today?"

Knowing better than to play dumb with Abby, Ellie nodded. But she didn't want to talk about Sloan.

"The same Sloan Cassidy that you spent so many months refusing to cry over during high school?"

Trust her sister to have such an acute memory. Abby, who was an obstetrician at Maitland Maternity, was one of the smartest women Ellie had ever known.

"That's him," she said now, trying for a nonchalant smile. If she acted like she didn't care, no one else would.

"What's he want?"

"Help with his kids."

Abby nodded, her eyes narrowing as she watched Ellie. "Your help?"

"Maybe," Ellie answered evasively. She didn't like the sudden light in Abby's eyes. Didn't trust it. Her sister might be intelligent, but she was also recently engaged and a bit loony with love.

Hoping to help Abby see sense, Ellie told her about Sloan's divorce, his current problem, and the impossible and completely inappropriate thing he'd asked of her.

Abby smiled, straightening in the doorway. "So you're going to help him?"

"No."

"Oh." Her older sister frowned. "Why not?"

"I don't have time." Ellie stated the obvious, leaving the less easily explained for herself. "How's Marcie and the baby?" she asked quickly, shameless in her attempt at diversion.

It was a testimony to how much in love Abby was that she allowed herself to be diverted. "Great," she answered with a grin. Abby had delivered her soon-to-be sister-in-law's baby the week before. "They're both home with Kyle, driving him crazy."

Ellie had heard that Abby was spending all her free time at her fiancé's house, as well. She'd never seen her sister so happy.

And as she went off to night class, she felt a little happier herself. It had taken Abby thirty-two years to find her happiness. Ellie still had lots of time.

SLOAN WAITED until the next morning to call her. But only because it took him that long to trust himself to do the right thing. He had to apologize. He'd had no business going to her—a Maitland—for help. She'd caught the fallout from a moment of weakness. And there was no excuse at all for the bullheadedness that hadn't allowed him to accept no for an answer.

But he was done with that now.

"Ellie, it's Sloan," he began as soon as he heard her voice on the line. "Wait!" he said a little too loudly. "Don't hang up, I just want to apologize."

"Apologize?"

She sounded as though that were the last thing she'd expect from him. "For imposing on you. I had no business bothering you with my problems."

"Apology accepted."

If he'd been hoping she'd changed her mind, he'd been a fool. But it wouldn't be the first time. Especially not where Miss Ellie Maitland was concerned. The woman made him crazy.

"Did you find a baby-sitter?" she asked, when he thought she'd probably hung up.

Tempted to just put an end to his misguided scheme, he almost lied to her. Almost.

"No."

"Oh."

There it was again. That note of longing in her voice.

An echo, he was certain, of the longing he'd seen in her eyes as she'd gazed at his adorable little hellions. Not that he trusted his judgment where Ellie was concerned. He was probably making it all up.

"I'm sorry I couldn't help, Sloan, but you came to the wrong person," she said as the silence grew too long again. "I know nothing about raising children."

If only her excuse was valid, then maybe he'd be able to let go. If only he didn't remember how grateful she'd been when he'd saved her from herself ten years before. If only he didn't remember the life he'd discovered all cooped up inside her. If only he hadn't kissed her that one time and ruined an incredible friendship...

"You're a natural with children, El. As I recall, you spent more of your teenage years with little kids than you did with your peers."

Sloan winced at his own words. What an incredibly asinine thing to remind her of—the fact that she'd been such a wallflower, she'd had to baby-sit to get out of the house. The worst thing was, she'd thought the fault had been hers, when, in fact, it had been exactly the opposite. The fault had been that of the ignorant and immature jerks in high school who hadn't been able to see past the baggy clothes and glasses to the shapely body and quick mind they'd hidden.

Only Sloan had seen. And Sloan hadn't been worthy of her incredible gifts.

Still wasn't.

"Yeah, well," she said after another long pause. "That was a long time ago. I've forgotten most of it."

Ariel's cup of milk hit Sloan in the head and burst open, spilling the thick white liquid down the side of his face and into the phone.

"What was that?" Ellie asked, just as Sloan cursed a blue, though whispered, streak.

"Ariel's counterattack for my having strapped her in her high chair," he said, as Alisha wound up, too. "No!" But as always, he was a fraction of a second too late. Alisha's aim wasn't quite as good. Her cup bounced off the cupboard before splashing milk all over the floor.

"I have to go, Ellie," Sloan said, beaten, attempting to wipe the milk from his ear.

"Yes, well, bring the kids to the clinic until you get a sitter, Sloan. Beth would be happy to have them in the day care."

"Thanks," Sloan said, ringing off just as a soggy piece of toast hit him in the chest. He didn't bother explaining to Ellie that he didn't need a baby-sitter. He needed a savior.

ELLIE DECIDED TO WALK home for dinner. The ten blocks between the clinic and Maitland Drive, where she grew up, weren't nearly enough to clear her mind, but the fresh October air invigorated her body. And the time alone was a balm.

An unfamiliar car was parked just down from Maitland Mansion's drive. Not that Ellie minded, but she had to veer around it. Only mildly curious, she continued through the black iron gates and slowly up the drive. She hoped Jessie, their cook, had made something light for dinner. Ellie didn't feel much like eating, and Megan was sure to notice if she just picked at her food.

Not for the first time, Ellie considered moving out, getting a place of her own.

She never would have noticed the woman partially concealed by the bushes on the west side of the four-story mansion that was her home if it hadn't been for the rays of the setting sun reflecting off the camera lens. *Chelsea Markum.*

Unfortunately for the rabid reporter, Ellie was in the mood for a fight.

Creeping slowly up behind her, Ellie ran through possible options for dealing with the determined woman. And froze when she caught a glimpse of Chelsea's prey: baby Cody was lying on a quilt in the middle of the downstairs living room, his little legs dancing in the air. Chelsea's video camera was pointed right at him.

"No!" Ellie sprang forward without thinking—an action as unlike her as the karate chop she landed on Chelsea's shoulder, causing the camera to slip from the startled woman's grasp. As the camera hit the ground, the film compartment fell open, spilling the video tape onto the ground.

Ellie stepped on it.

Her "Leave him alone" came out in a whisper as she looked down at what she'd done.

Chelsea, obviously as shocked as Ellie, stared from Ellie's face to the ground and back again, speechless. "You…you…"

"Just take the camera and go," Ellie said, tired and disarmed by actions so completely out of character. "I'd tell you you were trespassing, but you already know that. It's against the law," she heard herself continue. "You know that, too. Don't make me call the police."

"You can't hide this thing forever," the reporter said, picking up her camera. "Sooner or later we're going to find out who abandoned that baby. And when we do, you're going to wish you'd been a little more cooperative."

Watching the woman stride purposefully down the

drive, Ellie figured she should be upset by the veiled threat. Maybe she was.

At least she now knew who the unfamiliar car belonged to.

"HERE'S HOPING we're nobodies tonight," Megan told her twin daughters as they followed her into her bedroom suite to watch the ten o'clock news that night. The practice had become almost a ritual over the past month as they'd seen their name smeared across the state.

Baby Cody was asleep in his crib, his nurse in her room close by.

"You don't think she got anything today, do you?" Beth asked her mother, sitting cross-legged on the floor in front of the television. Newly engaged, Beth was admiring the diamond glittering on her finger.

Megan, dressed in a silk dressing gown that only emphasized her tall, regal stature, settled on the couch and shrugged. "We have no idea how long she was out there before Ellie caught her. She may have had more than one tape."

"The bitch," Beth murmured under her breath.

Ellie smiled at her twin, enjoying, as always, Beth's outspoken nature. Beth called it like she saw it. Ellie saw it, but hardly ever called anything.

Having gone back to the clinic after dinner, Ellie had just arrived home moments before and was still in the blue suit she'd worn to work that morning. She joined her mother on the couch.

"At least we weren't headlines," Megan said during the first commercial break.

Beth, her PJ's a pair of men's flannel underwear and a T-shirt, nodded. "Yeah, if she got anything good, we'd have been headlines."

Ellie had to agree. She asked her mother about the presidential battle that *had* made the headlines, and while Beth went into the bathroom, the two of them discussed politics until the news was back on.

They made it through the second commercial break, and Ellie breathed a sigh of relief. It was stupid, really, for her to be worrying about the effect all of this was going to have on the baby boy sleeping not too far away, especially after an entire month of ignoring his existence. Still, she couldn't seem to help herself. She felt suddenly protective of the little man—and concerned about his future.

Preparing to excuse herself, Ellie stood before the news was even over. It had been a long day; she was tired and had a load of homework to do to prepare for class the next week.

"…And now, with more on the Maitland baby scandal, we turn you over to *Tattle Today TV* reporter Chelsea Markum…"

Ellie froze.

"…You can't be an Austinite without being familiar with Maitland Drive, or with the maternity clinic for which the family has gained international recognition." A picture of Maitland Mansion flashed up on the screen, followed by another of Maitland Maternity Clinic. "But how long has it been since anyone has taken a look behind the family's public facade to find the flesh-and-blood people living within?

"Interest in the family has been rampant ever since the appearance of an unnamed Maitland heir on the clinic's doorstep last month. And though we're no closer to finding out who the baby's father is, we've discovered a few other secrets the Maitlands may prefer to hide. Why is it that twenty-five-year-old Ellie Maitland, toting only a bachelor's degree, was appointed administrator of the world-renowned clinic? Nepotism you might ask?''

"I guess I pissed her off.''

Megan grasped Ellie's hand, pulling her back down to the couch. Beth scooted over and leaned against Ellie's legs. Ellie concentrated on keeping her dinner down.

Chelsea continued, airing previously taped interviews with a couple of the clinic's business associates. Both of them men; both of them over fifty. Neither of them bothered to hide their disdain at the thought of taking their business to Ellie.

"I had occasion this week to discover a little bit more about this mysterious young woman who has single-handedly taken on the overwhelming responsibility of seeing to the safe running of a clinic whose clientele includes some of the world's most famous mothers and babies.''

"You are pretty awesome, El,'' Beth said, smiling up at her.

Megan squeezed the hand she still held.

With a photo of Ellie as backdrop, Chelsea Markum continued. "What I found wasn't all sunshine and roses. The Maitland Maternity administrator isn't always as caring and concerned as she would have us believe. A childhood friend—a very handsome, single male childhood friend—approached Ms. Maitland earlier this week, desperately in need of help with his motherless twin babies…''

Ellie's hands and feet began to tingle as Chelsea described the scene in her office with a completely uncomplimentary slant. She could hardly hear the reporter for the roaring in her ears. She'd gone to bed, was having a really bad dream.

"...while this may not be much in and of itself, when coupled with last month's abandoned baby, one can't help but wonder if, contrary to their PR, turning their backs on children in need is a family trait—"

"No!"

Ellie and Beth stared as their mother jumped up and, none too gently, turned off the television. "She's gone too far." Megan's words were clipped, furious, and she began to pace her suite.

Megan's reaction scared Ellie more than anything the reporter had said.

"Is it true?" Beth asked after a couple of moments.

Ellie felt, rather than saw, her mother's feet still.

"Sloan did come to my office," Ellie said. But she hadn't been as heartless as Chelsea Markum had painted her. Had she?

"And you refused to help him?" Megan asked quietly.

Looking up at her mother, Ellie wondered if this was the time when Megan would actually show her disappointment in her next-to-youngest daughter.

"I told him he could bring the babies to Beth until he could find a sitter."

"If all he needed was a baby-sitter, why'd he come to you?" Beth asked.

Ellie's gaze bounced between her mother and her twin. How could she help them understand what she didn't really understand herself? "He said he needed me, that he didn't so much want someone to watch the babies, but wanted to learn how to look after them himself. That's not something you have someone teach you," she said, looking at her mother beseechingly. "It's just something you do."

"Unless you don't know how," Megan said softly.

But her eyes were filled with compassion, not blame. "Looking after children came naturally to you, sweetie, but you've been around babies all your life. And grew up with brothers and sisters. What kind of example did Sloan have?"

None. Unless you could call a womanizing absentee father and an alcoholic mother role models.

Beth hugged her knees up to her chest, facing the couch where Ellie still sat. "He's got one hell of a lot of nerve coming to you," she said.

Ellie wanted to think so. She sat on the edge of the couch, her hands clasped between her knees.

"And yet, who more natural for him to come to than the only person who'd ever taken the time to get to know the boy inside the man?" Megan said. "Especially a woman who's a natural with children."

"I haven't held a baby in more than ten years," Ellie said. And then remembered. *At least, not until a couple of nights ago.* But one night of baby holding didn't count.

"Caring for children is not something you forget," Megan said gently.

"You think I should have told him I'd help?" Ellie asked, feeling like a little girl again, not wanting to disappoint her mother.

"Not necessarily," Megan replied, surprising her. "I'm just not sure I understand why you didn't."

"Because the jerk broke her heart!" Beth jumped up and faced her mother.

"They were friends, Beth. It's not his fault Ellie fell so deeply in love with him."

"That's ancient history." Ellie stood, too. She wasn't going to have them all feeling sorry for her again.

"Then why'd you say no?" Megan asked again.

"I don't have time."

The excuse embarrassed Ellie even as she said it. She was busy, yes, but if no one else knew that she kept herself busy on purpose, Megan did. Her mother knew how much extra work, over and above her duties, Ellie had been doing at the clinic.

Moving toward the bedroom half of the suite, Megan pulled down her comforter and fluffed the pillows on her side of the bed. "Life's short, El," she said.

Ellie's gaze wandered over to the side of the bed that had remained undisturbed every single night since her father's death. It was almost as though the empty space offered some kind of comfort to her widowed mother, a testimony to the man who still owned the empty places in Megan's heart.

"You think I should help him," Ellie said.

"I don't," Beth protested. "At least, not if you don't want to."

"I think you should do what you feel is right, Ellie. Just make sure you know what it is you really feel."

Her mother made it sound so easy.

## CHAPTER FOUR

TIPTOEING PAST the nurse's open door, Ellie slid into the nursery, unable to fight the urge to make this nocturnal visit. She hadn't seen baby Cody up close since she'd held him the other night. But since she'd caught Chelsea spying on him, she'd needed to connect. To assure herself that he really was just fine.

To find out why he was pulling at her all of a sudden.

He didn't have any answers for her.

"I have to help Sloan just to shut up the press, to protect the family's reputation," she whispered softly to the sleeping baby. Cody found the excuse so flimsy that he didn't even bother to acknowledge that she'd spoken, she thought wryly. Not with so much as a puckering of his baby brow. "Okay," she continued softly, "part of me wants to help him." She held her breath, waiting to see if the announcement garnered any reaction. It didn't.

Breathing a sigh of relief when Cody didn't move, Ellie relaxed a bit. The truth wasn't so shocking, after all. "There will have to be stipulations, of course," she told the baby, her voice gathering confidence, if not volume. "I'll only be able to offer whatever spare time I have. This can't interfere in any way with my job at the clinic. With my long-term goals."

Cody didn't disagree. His little tummy still rose and fell methodically with every breath he took. Ellie knelt down beside the crib, resting one hand on the baby's mattress.

"And I will in no way delude myself as to Sloan's feelings for me this time," she told him categorically. They had to be very clear on this point. "Loving him the first time almost killed me."

With a deep release of breath she hadn't known she'd been holding, Ellie sat down on her heels. It felt damn good to finally get that confession off her chest.

"You probably haven't figured all of us out yet, but I'm pretty uptight as people go." Confessing felt so good, she couldn't seem to stop. "I tend to be serious—not fun and sexy like Beth."

Stopping to make certain that the baby wasn't paying attention, that she wasn't hurting his sensibilities by mentioning the sex thing, Ellie watched his little lashes where they lay against his cheek. He was so beautiful. So innocent and trusting.

As were the little imps Sloan had had propped against his hips the other day.

"I'm not going to fall in love with him again," she told the sleeping infant. "Men like Sloan aren't attracted to women like me—but that's okay," she added hurriedly. "I'm at peace with that. I have my family—which includes you, little man—and I have my job, which I love. Together you all make up the solid foundation upon which my life is based…"

By the time Ellie finally returned to her bed, the night was half gone. But she spent the remainder of it enjoying a surprisingly peaceful sleep.

SARA WALKED QUIETLY through the administrative department of Maitland Maternity, only vaguely aware of the hot take-out container warming her hands. Her boss, Shelby Lord, had asked her to deliver breakfast to R. J. Maitland, and she was going to do just that, in spite of the fact that the billionaire family intimidated the hell out of her.

His secretary's desk was empty. Shelby had said all she had to do was leave the eggs Benedict with Dana Dillinger. She hadn't said the woman might not be at her desk.

Damn. Now what did she do?

Looking from the warm container—which wasn't going to be warm indefinitely—to the cracked door of the president's office, Sara shifted her weight from foot to foot.

She might not know much at the moment, but she was fairly certain that R. J. Maitland wasn't going to be too happy with cold eggs. She'd only been at the diner next door for a couple of days, but she'd already heard enough about the workaholic eldest Maitland sibling to know that much. She knew, also, that she needed her job—desperately. At the moment, it was all she had.

"Excuse me, sir?" She pushed open the door.

R. J. Maitland, bent over his desk, didn't even look up.

"I've brought your breakfast," Sara tried again.

He continued to scribble something across the page in front of him.

Not knowing what else to do, and fretting about the customers and tips she was missing back at the diner, Sara tiptoed forward, placed the container on his desk.

"Thank you." The words were slightly muffled, aimed as they were toward the desk.

"You're welcome," she said automatically.

She left the room as quickly as she'd come, pretty

sure that R. J. Maitland didn't even know she'd been there. For all the attention he'd paid her, he'd probably thought she was his secretary—the woman who delivered his food to his desk on a fairly regular basis, from what Sara had heard.

Hey, for all she knew, maybe she'd been a secretary, too. Maybe she knew all about delivering take-out cartons of food to a boss without disturbing him.

Still on the second floor, which housed the administrative offices, Sara heard a baby cry and stopped, her heart almost beating out of her chest. She leaned against the wall, hoping no one was coming, telling herself she'd be okay and trying to breathe. She heard it—the baby was still crying. And suddenly, so was Sara.

What was the matter with her?

Trembling, she clung to the wall for support, reaching deep inside herself for whatever well of strength had seen her through the last couple of weeks.

"Sara?"

The voice was familiar. Friendly. *Ellie.*

"Are you okay?"

"I will be." She straightened, smiled at Ellie, wiped away her tears. She'd liked the serious—inded woman when they'd met the other day. She'd felt safe when Ellie was near.

"You sure?" Ellie asked, her eyes filled with compassion, and more. There was a quiet strength about Ellie Maitland that made Sara feel as though she could rely on her for anything.

Even picking up the pieces of a broken life. If she asked Ellie to help her, Sara knew somehow that the other woman wouldn't stop until she'd found Sara's answers—no matter how long it took.

"I'm sure," Sara said, finding a smile. She couldn't

ask someone as important as Ellie Maitland for help. But it sure felt good to know that the woman was close by, if Sara ever reached the point where she couldn't carry on another day. The thought gave her strength.

"We could sit for a minute if you'd like, or I can call a nurse."

Shaking her head, Sara felt her strength returning. "I'm fine, really," she insisted, anxious now to get back to her customers. Her tips. "It was just weird there for a minute. I heard a baby cry and I just—I don't know, I lost it for a second."

Frowning, Ellie studied her. "Were you maybe remembering something?"

The possibility had crossed her mind. The feeling had been so strong, so devastating. "Nothing but a feeling, if I was," she said.

A feeling she was petrified to trace. What awful things were lurking in the darkness of her locked-up mind?

"I guess I better get back to the diner," she said, before Ellie could pursue the conversation.

"If you ever need to talk, my office is right down the hall."

Though she couldn't imagine taking Ellie up on the offer, Sara was warmed by it just the same.

"DA-EE, UP!"

"No, Alisha, I'm changing Ariel," Sloan explained to the toddler tugging on the leg of his jeans.

"Da-ee up!" Alisha demanded a second time, her voice starting to tremble and gain volume both at the same time.

"Alisha, Daddy's changing Ariel," he said, trying to reason with her. "I can't pick you up right now."

Keeping both of his hands firmly on the baby squirming on the change table, Sloan spared a quick glance for the little girl clutching his leg with pasty fingers.

"Da-ee, up!" Alisha wailed.

Sloan picked her up.

"You ever gonna learn to stick to your guns?" Charlie asked from the doorway of Ariel's room.

Damn. Sloan hadn't known Charlie had arrived yet that morning. It was humiliating having the older man see him make such a mess of things.

"I stick to my guns on the things that matter," Sloan said. He just couldn't think of what mattered that much at the moment.

So here he was, one daughter sucking her thumb in his ear, the other rolling over, half dressed, on the table in front of him, and his housekeeper shaking his head as if Sloan were the biggest loser on the face of the earth.

Unwilling to have Charlie witness the uproar if he attempted to finish dressing Ariel, Sloan picked up the diaper-clad infant and pretended that he'd meant to take one half-naked daughter to breakfast. At least Ariel was halfway ready. Alisha was still in her pajamas, having thrown such a fit when Sloan had laid her down to change her that he'd decided to give it a rest and tackle Ariel first.

He was saved from further admonitions when the phone rang, and Charlie went to answer it. He hoped whoever it was would keep his housekeeper busy for half an hour at least. It was going to take Sloan that long to convince his darling daughters to sit in their high chairs for breakfast.

"It's for you—I'll take them," Charlie said, back in the doorway.

Sloan would have argued, but he knew better. As he handed the girls over, he also knew that he could be on the phone five minutes and return to find Charlie with both girls dressed, strapped in high chairs and happily eating Cheerios.

"Sloan Cassidy here," he said, picking up the phone in the office, oddly ashamed at the relief he felt now that he'd escaped to his haven.

"It's Ellie."

His heart dropped. And then sped up double-time. In all his life, he suddenly realized, there'd never been any time he'd felt happier than during those hours he'd spent with Ellie in high school. "I'm glad you called," he said. It was the first thing that came to mind.

"I'm not agreeing to anything, Sloan, so don't run with this or anything, but what exactly did you have in mind when you asked for my help?"

*Don't run with it.* He silently repeated her warning, but it was no good. He was dashing all over the countryside. "There are times when I need to go places with the girls and could sure use a companion to help with double car seats, double spilled food, double tears," he said, thinking *for starters*.

That was the easy part.

"I can't guarantee I'd be available whenever you have to go somewhere."

"Even some of the time would be great," he hurriedly assured her. "Even one time would be heaven."

"They're that much trouble?"

He hadn't been talking about the girls.

"They're a handful, at least when I'm around." And the way he remembered it from high school, he'd always felt stronger, more capable of coping when Ellie was there. She just had a way of making things seem manageable, and, Lord knew, he could use managing.

"They're different when you're not around?" she asked, homing right in on the problem, as Ellie always had.

"So I'm told." So he knew. He could hear Charlie in the kitchen already, pouring cereal. Which meant the girls were in their high chairs, right where they belonged.

"Why?"

Sinking into the big leather chair behind his desk, Sloan turned and looked out the picture window at his ranch. Cattle, tornadoes, squatters, he could handle. Baby girls, he could not. "That's what I really need your help on," he admitted. "I need you to teach me how to be a father, or a mother, or any kind of parent at all."

The admission should have been humiliating, but with Ellie, it wasn't.

"I'm hardly an expert," she warned.

"I took them to the zoo." Sloan heard himself recounting one of his worst nightmares. "Neither of them would sit in their stroller. But when I tried to carry them, they kicked and squirmed to get down. I put them down—they're both walking now—and they wouldn't hold my hands. Thankfully they were distracted by a cotton candy vendor. I bought some for them, but they refused to sit down to eat it. Ariel threw hers and hit me in the chest with it. Alisha just cried all over hers. The animals ran scared, and everyone was looking at me like I was some kind of demon. I finally had to leave with them screaming so loud all the way out to the car, I'm surprised someone didn't call protective services."

He wasn't sure, but he thought Ellie was laughing.

"It wasn't funny," he said, breaking out in a sweat just thinking about the awful day.

"Ever thought of not giving them everything they ask for?" she finally said, her humor, if it had been there, under control.

"I don't."

"Okay, so when do we start?"

Wanting to pin her down before she had a second to change her mind, he asked, "Is tomorrow too soon? We have eighteen—onth well-baby checks, and I won't even bother to tell you how awful the last doctor visit was."

"What time?" Ellie asked, all businesslike.

Sloan looked up the appointment on his calendar, and Ellie said she would take a late lunch to accommodate him.

He hung up as soon as he'd made plans to pick her up at the clinic shortly after one. And the only reason he suddenly felt fifty pounds lighter was that he finally had some help with his burden. It had nothing whatsoever to do with the fact that he had Ellie Maitland back in his life again.

He was an adult now, his self-control well and truly tested. He wouldn't make hash of the friendship as he had in high school. Wouldn't tarnish it, or Ellie, by giving in to his baser appetites. She was going to help him with his girls. Period.

He wasn't going to repeat old mistakes.

ELLIE OFTEN RETURNED to her office at the clinic after dinner, and, that's exactly where Lana Lord found her that night.

"Beth said you weren't going with us to the premiere tonight," Lana announced from the doorway, bypassing a hello.

Shaking her head, Ellie spared her good friend a smile and a look of regret, then finished typing the sentence she'd left dangling on her computer screen. She typed fast, though, wanting to chat with Lana. Tonight her friend was dressed in a black jumpsuit that made the reddish highlights in her hair look like flames. She sat down in front of Ellie's desk and waited patiently. Ellie dashed a couple more sentences off, feeling decidedly underdressed in her day old brown business suit.

When Ellie looked up again, Lana was fiddling with a big blue bow on the little package she'd brought with her. She didn't look happy.

"Sorry," Ellie said, afraid that if she didn't make some deposits with her friends soon, she was going to find herself without any.

"No problem." Lana grinned. "I've loved you for as long as I can remember, so I'm used to you. Besides, you've got so many great qualities. I'd be a fool not to overlook a fault or two."

Lana's saucy smile always lit up her face. "Yeah?" Ellie asked, smiling back. "So what are these great qualities?" Not usually one to seek out praise, Ellie couldn't seem to help herself. She was feeling really vulnerable with the change she'd just made in her life: the decision to step outside her routine and help Sloan. To risk.

"You're strong."

"That's it?" If that was all, she was in trouble. She didn't feel strong at all.

"Of course not," Lana said, becoming serious, "Ellie, you're the best friend a person could have. You may not always have a lot of time for fun, but when I need you, you're there. Without fail. You're loyal and thoughtful. You've never forgotten my birthday, and you've been there for every momentous happening in my life. You're that way with all of us. You have a way of making a person feel safe, cared for, important."

"Whoa!" Ellie said, studying her friend through a film of tears. "You'd better stop before I get a big head. We both know I'm boring and far too serious."

"It's your seriousness that makes you so reliable," Lana said. "I can always trust you to see things as they are, and to help me see them that way. You can handle anything. And you aren't the least bit boring. I wish I knew half the stuff you do!"

"And I wish I knew half the things you do," Ellie told her friend. She wished she had Lana's easy confidence, her lighthearted way of approaching life.

"Think we could get a brain switch in Mitch's laboratory?" Lana asked, drawing the last word out eerily, as though she were suggesting stepping into a Frankenstein movie.

Ellie grinned. "I wouldn't want to chance it. We might end up pregnant."

"God forbid." Lana's expression held just enough horror to be comical.

"So who's the present for?" Ellie asked.

"Baby Cody." Lana handed over the package hesitantly.

"You want to talk about it?"

"The present?" Lana shrugged, her green eyes troubled. "It's a teddy bear teething ring, no big deal." Lana ran a store that carried everything that a baby could ever need, and since Cody's appearance, she'd been bringing the baby gifts on an almost daily basis.

Ellie came around her desk, leaning back against it. "Not the present—the baby," she guessed.

She could almost see the thoughts spinning around

in Lana's head. The defensiveness, the fear—the vulnerability. After all, she and Lana had been friends for a
long time.

Lana looked up, meeting Ellie's gaze. She didn't have
to say anything. Ellie knew. "It's really getting to you,
isn't it—the abandonment?"

"I just don't get how a woman could carry a baby
inside her body for nine months, birth that baby, and
then throw it away!" she cried. Her voice carried down
the empty halls of the administrative wing, her pain
echoing back into the room.

"I know."

"It's not natural." Lana's eyes begged her to understand.

"I know."

"He's just an innocent little baby, and his life is already tarnished. This is something he'll have to take
with him, that will bother him for the rest of his life."

"I know," Ellie said again softly, watching her friend.
"I didn't get it before."

Tears brimmed at the edges of Lana's eyes as she
looked up questioningly.

"I never really understood just how much you hurt,
knowing that your mother left the four of you on our
doorstep. I mean, I just always thought that if she had
to give you up, it was pretty damn decent of her to pick
such a perfect place."

Lana said nothing, just shook her head, obviously
aching.

"I was always so aware that if she hadn't left you, we
wouldn't have met, grown up together," she continued.
"You four wouldn't have been adopted by the Lords.
You wouldn't have had such cool parents, so many ad-
vantages." Ellie shook her head at her own naiveté. As
if money could buy happiness.

"And when you wake up in the middle of the night," Lana explained, "and everyone's asleep and you're all alone in the world and afraid that it will be that way forever, you can't help but wonder why you weren't special enough to hold on to the one basic thing most people take for granted—your mother's unconditional love." A tear spilled over, dripped down her cheek.

"It kills me to think of you suffering like that," Ellie admitted to her friend. "And I can't bear to think of baby Cody ever feeling that way."

Lana blinked, startled. "Beth told me you haven't had a thing to do with the baby."

Shrugging, Ellie confessed to her best friend what she'd been unable to admit to anyone else. "I've been into his room at night. I know I have no reason to, but I feel so protective of him. I stand and look at him sleeping so innocently, or pick him up and feel his warmth, and it just makes me want to cry. I mean, he's being very well cared for, even loved already. If he stays with us, he'll have the best life can give him, emotionally as well as monetarily, but still, knowing that his mother just up and deserted him hurts so much."

Lana smiled, reached for Ellie's hand and squeezed it. "You do understand. Having you next door, being my friend, living with the Lords were all great things, Ellie. You all taught me that you don't have to be related by blood ties to be a family."

"So if Cody turns out not to be ours, we can teach him that, too?" Ellie asked quietly, taking comfort in the reassurance of her friend's touch.

"Is that what you're afraid of? That he won't be a Maitland?"

"It would be so much better for him if he is."

"Probably."

"But I can't stand to think that one of my brothers was so irresponsible—so cold and selfish and heartless—to desert his own child."

"Maybe he doesn't know."

"Maybe." Ellie fervently hoped that was the case, if indeed it turned out that one of her brothers was Cody's father. "And maybe, when he finds out he's the dad, Cody will have his happily ever after."

"You really do care an awful lot about that baby, don't you?"

Ellie nodded.

"I'm glad. You're finally reaching out, coming back to life."

Wait until Lana heard how far she was reaching. "Sloan Cassidy is back."

Stiffening, Lana dropped Ellie's hand. "I didn't know he'd gone anywhere."

"Back in my life."

"Is that wise?" Lana had made no attempt to hide her disdain for the man over the years. She blamed Sloan for creating Ellie's workaholic tendencies.

"Marla left him."

"Pity."

"With eighteen—onth-old twins. Girls."

"Wow."

"Yeah, and apparently he's not doing such a bang-up job of raising them."

"Surprise, surprise."

Ellie grinned in spite of herself. "Give him a break, Lan. He couldn't help that I didn't light his spark."

"He's an idiot."

"I've agreed to help him with the girls."

"You're an idiot."

"Probably." Ellie conceded the truth, but still needed

her friend to understand. "Have you met Shelby's new waitress yet?" she asked.

"The amnesiac?"

"Yeah, Sara."

"I met her the other day. She seems really sweet, poor thing."

"I met her, too," Ellie said, frowning. She wondered if Lana would think she was as crazy as her words were going to sound. "And I felt like she and I had a lot in common."

Lana's brows came together as she stared up at Ellie. "I don't follow you."

"Her life is completely empty, Lana." Ellie paused, then swallowed. "Mine is, too."

Silence filled the room as the two women communicated the understanding and compassion that had seen them through all of life's heartaches and disappointments together.

"Be careful?" Lana finally whispered.

Too choked up to speak, Ellie nodded.

"You really fell hard last time, El."

"I know."

"He's a natural charmer."

Nodding, Ellie smiled sadly. "I know."

"Women always flocked to him in droves."

"I know."

Lana's eyes looked pained again. She took a deep breath, as though facing an unpleasant task. "No matter how great a friend he is, Ellie, he goes for women like Marla."

*Women like Beth,* Ellie supplied for herself. *Fun, easygoing, sexy women.*

"I know."

## CHAPTER FIVE

THE DOCTOR'S OFFICE was far too crowded. Grumpy children filled the waiting room with their coughs and sniffles—and occasional noisy outbursts. Actually, in fairness to the roomful of kids, Ellie had to concede that it was only Sloan's two who were guilty of noisy outbursts. The rest just whined and wiped their runny noses on a sleeve—sometimes their own, sometimes not.

Ellie, sitting in one of the few unslobbered-upon chairs, watched from a distance as Sloan sat cross-legged on the floor, attempting to keep his offspring from springing off.

"Mine!" Alisha grabbed for the book Sloan had been attempting to read to the girls.

Ariel watched her sister vie for the book for a moment, and then half crawled, half walked over to grab a dirty building block and lift it to her drooling mouth.

"No!" Sloan cried, a bit louder than he probably should have, and grabbed the grubby toy before it reached its mark.

"Mine!" Ariel screamed, and promptly burst into tears. At which point Ellie tried to hide behind her hand, while every other parent in the room stared.

"Mine!" Alisha cried again, reaching for the book Sloan still, by some miracle, held in his hand.

"Okay, okay," he said, bending toward Alisha. "You

can have the book if you promise to sit right here next to Daddy and read it. Okay?''

"'Kay," Alisha said, sniffling pathetically.

Sloan waited for the little girl to plop back down next to him. She didn't.

"Mine!" Ariel was still crying, reaching for the block.

"Mine!" Alisha said, gearing up for another spate of tears.

Tempted to step in and resolve the whole situation, Ellie forced herself to sit back. On the way over, Sloan had asked that she just observe at first, get to know the girls, see if she could tell what he was doing wrong.

She wondered how long he wanted the list to be.

"Here, have it," Sloan said suddenly, giving the book to Alisha. With the book in hand, Alisha crawled away toward a fish tank that was set up by the receptionist's desk. Using the wall to right herself, she looked up at the tank.

Ellie looked at Sloan, waiting for him to rescue the fish tank and then take the book away from the child, since she hadn't kept her side of the bargain they'd made. A bargain she was really too young to understand.

Sloan was too busy making another deal over a block—something about sitting quietly while it was washed—with Ariel. One that Ellie was fairly certain wasn't going to be kept, either. Ariel was showing no signs of wanting to sit, or be quiet.

Ellie jumped up and grabbed Alisha before she could do real damage to herself, or the poor fish that were her target. The book wasn't so lucky. The baby managed, as she squirmed in Ellie's arms, to toss the book into the tank—where it sank, ruined, to the bottom.

Sloan was still trying to bribe Ariel into silence

by walking down the hall with her to buy chocolate candies from a vending machine.

"THOSE CLINIC PEOPLE probably shouldn't have candy in a doctor's office," Ellie said when they were finally back in Sloan's super cab truck and on their way to Maitland Maternity. The exhausted toddlers were both asleep in their car seats.

"They shouldn't have dirt there, either," Sloan grunted.

He looked more in need of a nap than his daughters.

"They also shouldn't make you wait so long. Any kid would get restless after an hour of that."

Falling into old habits, Ellie needed, first and foremost, to make him feel better. She wasn't going to lie to him or give him some big snow job. A lot of the problem back there had been him. But he hadn't been the only problem. The cards had been stacked against him.

And his pride was the easiest thing to fix.

"Ford Carrington's the pediatrician at the clinic," she said tentatively, afraid to overstep her boundaries. Especially since she still wasn't really clear, even in her mind, just what those boundaries were.

Sloan grunted.

"He's so gentle with the kids, it makes your heart break."

"You think I should change doctors?" Sloan asked, sending her a glance that melted her insides.

"It would be a start."

"Is this Carrington guy taking new patients?"

Ford was incredibly busy just keeping up with the babies born at the clinic. But he worked for her. "I'm sure he'd have room for Ariel and Alisha."

Sending her another glance, one that told her he was no fool, Sloan nodded. But he looked relieved as he said, "I'll arrange the necessary paperwork."

"Good." Ellie made a mental note to do her own footwork to ensure that Sloan's way was made easy.

And hoped she wasn't making the biggest mistake of her life.

KNOWING THAT HE'D KEPT her away from work longer than she'd intended that afternoon, Sloan played a hunch and called Ellie at the clinic after dinner that night. He wasn't surprised when she answered on the first ring. He felt guilty as hell for having been the cause of her late night.

"Should I call later?" he asked, the minute he heard her voice. And then kicked himself. If he was going to feel so bad about bothering her, why had he called her at all?

Because he was a damn fool and couldn't stop thinking about her. That was why.

"No bother," she said. "I'm just getting ready to go home."

She didn't sound angry or, worse, disgusted.

He'd been worried ever since he'd dropped her off earlier that afternoon about how poor an impression he and his troops had made. He'd been half listening for a call from her ever since, telling him that she'd changed her mind about helping him.

"So, what do you think?" he asked. Might as well get it all out in the open.

"About something in particular, or are we speaking generalities?"

Sloan grinned and leaned back against the pile of pillows bunched up against his headboard, left over from the night before. He couldn't remember the last time he'd made his bed.

"I'm taking a big risk here, I know, but what do you think of the girls?"

"They're intelligent, well fed, in good health—"

"I get the picture," he interrupted, afraid that her adjectives were going to go downhill. He raised one denim-clad knee, tapping his thumb against it. "So what about their father?"

"He's intelligent, not starving, appears to be in good health…"

Sloan chuckled. "I'd forgotten how good it was to talk to you."

"I hadn't."

Sloan slid his stockinged foot back down on the unmade king-size bed, thinking anew just how much he'd missed her. "I'm sorry things got so tangled up back then, El."

"I know. There's no need for an apology." Her voice changed, as though she didn't want to be having this particular conversation. Which strengthened his resolve to make certain that he didn't let things get screwed up again. No matter how great it felt being around her once more. He just had to keep his hands off her, and they'd be fine.

"So you think you can help me?" he finally said, not knowing what else to do but get back to business. He had a feeling he'd hurt her more than he'd realized back in high school. But he'd saved her from a lifetime of heartache, too. She just didn't know that.

"Depends on how thick your hide is."

Charlie's diatribes came instantly to mind. "Tough enough."

"You've got a lot to learn."

Something else he'd always appreciated about Ellie. Her honesty. "I'm a good student."

"I remember."

Their love of books had brought them together in the beginning. They'd been the only two in their crowd who'd seen the inherent value in doing homework.

"So we didn't scare you off?" Sloan asked, afraid to remember much more.

"I do what I say I'm going to do," Ellie said.

He knew that. He could count on her. Always had been able to. That was why he'd gone to her in the first place. "I owe you, big time."

"Yep."

He should have been worried at the promise to collect that he heard in her voice. But as he hung up the phone and lay there long enough for his aroused body to settle back down, Sloan couldn't muster up anything but a smile.

He was already looking forward to the next time he'd see her—and imagining ways in which she'd make him pay.

It wasn't until he remembered the reason for their parting ten years ago that his body finally minded his bidding and went limp.

THE HOTEL WASN'T AS SEEDY as the last one she'd hidden out in, but it sure as hell wasn't The Ritz. Janelle chomped on her gum as she applied fresh makeup, waiting for Petey to get out of the shower so they could go out and celebrate. Everything was finally ready. He was ready. It was only a matter of days now before she had what was rightfully hers.

Or, at least, the first handful. By this time next week, she was going to be living in style. Maitland style. And the greatest part was, they wouldn't even know what hit them.

Deftly she applied the deep red lipstick she preferred and smacked her gum once more for good measure. Yeah, screwing them right under their noses was almost the best part. Almost, but not quite. The money still won out. Money always would.

AT MEGAN'S INSTIGATION, Ellie invited Sloan and the twins over for a barbecue on the weekend. The October weather was lovely and warm, and the mansion grounds were perfect for two little bundles of energy. Ellie kind of liked the idea of spending time with the Cassidys while having her family around to protect her. It felt safer.

Beth had Cody and was out shopping, and Megan wasn't yet home from the clinic when Sloan and the girls arrived just after naptime on Saturday. Ellie heard him drive up. Actually, she'd seen his truck through the curtain she'd been hiding behind, but she waited for Harold, the Maitlands' butler, to let them in.

"Hi," she said, coming casually into the room after they were announced. She hoped the hour she'd taken choosing just the right pair of slacks and button-down blouse had the desired no-trouble-taken effect. She was certain her dark hair, with its blunt cut, screamed the message. It always did.

"This is more incredible than I'd imagined," Sloan said, grasping a pink-overalled baby to each hip as though they were holding him up. The girls, a bit intimidated by the unfamiliar surroundings, were sitting quietly on their perches, for once.

"Let's take them out back where they can get down and play," Ellie said, leading the way through the house to the backyard. "Jessie, our cook, is waiting for Mom to get here before she lights the grill."

Following her through the house, Sloan whistled as he caught a glimpse of the formal dining room.

"I can't believe you grew up like this."

Ellie shrugged. "You knew where we lived." Not that it had seemed to impress Sloan much. That had been one of the many things she'd liked about him.

"My imagination didn't do it justice."

"Would it have made a difference?"

Ellie held open the door for him as he walked out back with the girls. He settled them in the middle of the yard, between the guest cottage and the tennis courts, and tossed them a couple of balls and dolls from the bag on his shoulder before joining Ellie on the porch.

"It would have mattered, but it wouldn't have made a difference," he answered, as though the conversation had never been interrupted.

While Jessie went to get them glasses of fresh-squeezed lemonade, Ellie pondered his remark. And pondered him, too. This was the first time she'd ever seen him in her home. The mansion would never be the same again. His big, lean body filled up the space, giving it an energy, an excitement she'd never before found here.

"Why would it have mattered, and how could it then not make a difference?" she asked, once the cook had brought their drinks and gone back to her kitchen.

Sloan settled back in his chair, wondering how much to tell her. And knew that he'd tell her whatever she wanted to know. The rapport that had been so natural between them ten years ago was present again, as though they'd never been apart.

So, unfortunately, was the attraction. The curves she

hid underneath those serviceable clothes still drove him to distraction. But then, that was his curse in life: to be driven to distraction by a woman's curves. Any woman. Every woman.

"Did you know I used to lie awake nights and worry about how it looked—my being friends with you when we came from such different social worlds?" he asked, scooting down in his padded lawn chair until his head rested along the top of the cushion.

"You did not."

He watched her take a sip from the glass she held between two slender hands. He wouldn't bother to mention the nights he'd lain awake thinking about those hands on him.

Back then. And more recently.

"I did," he answered honestly. "You were a well-to-do goddess—the daughter of Austin's most beautiful couple. And I was the dusty and destitute son of a man who couldn't keep his body parts away from anything female and a woman who couldn't keep her mouth off a bottle."

"I was no goddess," Ellie objected. "You must be remembering Beth."

Sloan could have argued that point, but thought it was probably safer not to.

"So why did you bother with me at all?" she asked softly, breaking the silence that had fallen.

Sloan took his gaze away from his daughters, who were toddling their way across the yard toward him, to look at Ellie. "Because your friendship meant more to me than what people thought."

He noticed she couldn't tear her gaze away from his children at all.

"I'd like to believe that," she said, staring out at the yard.

Only the way Ellie kept rubbing at the condensation on her glass gave him any clue that they weren't just making small talk.

A quick glance at his daughters told him he didn't have much time. "You're probably the only real friend I've ever had." He wished he could have told her that ten years ago.

"Then why—"

"Ariel, no!" Sloan jumped up just as the little girl raised the baby doll she'd been carrying to whack her sister over the head—

Too late. Alisha screamed as though she'd been beheaded, and Ariel, watching her curiously, raised her arm a second time.

"Give me that," Sloan said, grabbing the doll just in time. "You don't hit your sister."

"Lisha cry," Ariel said, pointing toward the toddler. As Sloan would have reached for his unhappy offspring, Ellie scooped her up, cuddling her. Alisha's cries stopped almost instantly.

"Dowwy," Ariel demanded, pointing at the doll Sloan still held.

"No. You hit your sister with it. You can't play with it anymore."

Falling down hard to her bottom, Ariel's face puckered up, and Sloan's stomach dropped. He knew what was coming. And how long it would take him to get the child in good spirits again. He also knew how to prevent the disaster.

He handed her the doll.

ELLIE WAS STILL THINKING about Saturday afternoon with Sloan as she sat at her desk after hours on Monday. Everyone on the second floor had already left for the day, but Ellie didn't feel lonely; rather, she was glad for some time alone.

She couldn't figure out how a man as intelligent as Sloan could have such little confidence in his parenting skills. That he loved his girls was obvious. He watched them like a hawk, tended to their welfare. He did fall down a bit when it came to discipline. Setting limits and sticking to them. Even though the girls were little more than babies, they were obviously clever and needed more consistency from their father.

And what was that bit about her friendship meaning so much to him? He'd left her high and dry ten years ago.

She also couldn't figure out how, after all this time, after the callous way he'd kissed her senseless and then dumped her, she could still feel so alive just because he was in the room.

Fervently praying that her goals would stand her in good stead, that she had grown up, learned from experience, Ellie forced herself to concentrate on the work in front of her. Her only concern was to be the best damn administrator Maitland Maternity had ever seen. She couldn't let her mother and the rest of her family down. Especially not because of a man who'd made it humiliatingly, unforgettably clear long ago that he didn't want her.

Thinking she heard voices down the hall, Ellie was pulled from her nonproductive reverie. She'd thought she was upstairs alone. Who would be down by her mother's office?

Her first instinct was to call Security immediately.

But with all the recent publicity she'd been getting about her lack of experience, she decided to check things out herself. She would feel mighty foolish calling Security if it turned out to be R.J. working late as usual.

Ellie proceeded cautiously out the door of her office and slid along the wall, feeling like someone in a bad spy movie. Her chest was tight and her heart pounding as she moved slowly toward the voices. Or voice. A man's tenor was rumbling softly—too softly for Ellie to make out any words. She didn't think she recognized the voice.

Who was he talking to? And why?

Megan's office door was open. The light on. Ellie's heart pounded harder. What was happening in there? Was someone trying to steal from them?

Ellie was just thanking God that her mother was at home with Beth, when she heard Megan gasp. She ran the last few yards to the office door, and arrived just in time to see Megan collapse into the arms of a man Ellie had never seen before in her life.

"Who are you? What have you done?" Ellie demanded, rushing to her mother's side.

Before the man could do more than look up at Ellie, Megan straightened and stepped back from the stranger.

It was then that Ellie noticed the rumpled letter still clutched in her mother's hand. Megan recovered and quickly put it on the desk behind her. Though she stood on her own, she looked as though she'd seen a ghost— and was white enough to be one.

"Mother?" Ellie said, frightened.

"Ellie!" Megan's voice cracked. "What are you doing here?"

Her mother didn't look particularly happy to see her.

In fact, Ellie thought, her mother looked downright guilty. And horribly upset, as well. And maybe, though it made no sense at all, a little bit wonderstruck.

The expressions flickered across Megan's ashen face—a confusing conglomerate.

"Are you okay?" Ellie asked, her gaze shooting from her mother to the man, who still had one hand on her arm, and back again. "What's going on here? Who's he?"

She studied the stranger. He was tall, almost too good-looking in a weathered way, with dark hair and blue eyes that were daring her to find fault with him. He kind of reminded her of Sloan, with his outdoorsy cowboy look and big build, but there the resemblance ended. The look in Sloan's eyes spoke volumes.

Megan was looking at the man, too. Staring at him. She still hadn't answered Ellie's questions.

"I've got some business with your mother," the man finally said, offering Ellie his large, calloused hand.

She took it, trying desperately to size him up, to find any sense of normalcy in this bizarre situation. "I'm Ellie Maitland."

"Ellie, I—" Megan broke off, looking back and forth between Ellie and the stranger. She was frightening Ellie all over again. Ellie had never seen her mother at a loss for words.

Megan's eyes filled with tears.

"Mom?" Helping her mother to a seat, Ellie shot a murderous look at the stranger. What had he done to her?

Taking a deep breath, Megan looked at Ellie as she kneeled at her mother's feet. She took both of Ellie's hands between her own.

"I have something to tell you," Megan began,

"something that's difficult for me to talk about." She glanced at the man behind Ellie, smiled tremulously, unbelievingly, then turned her gaze back on Ellie. "It's something that you must promise me you'll keep between us until I have time to figure out how I'm going to tell the others."

Ellie nodded. Under the circumstances, what else could she do? She felt as cold as her mother's hands. Tears still trembled on Megan's lashes.

"You children all know that I was working as a maid for the Maitlands when I met your father," she started, her voice shaky. "My father, a widower, was a groundskeeper at Maitland Mansion, and it was through him that I got the job."

Ellie's gaze never left her mother's face, though so far, Megan had said nothing that Ellie hadn't already heard many times before. It was the faraway, pained look in her eyes that kept Ellie frozen. At the moment, Ellie was only vaguely aware of the stranger standing silently somewhere out of her sight.

"I—" Megan broke off, looked down. "I'm sorry. This is difficult for me."

"Mother?" Ellie asked, her stomach knotted with fear. "What's wrong? Are you ill?"

The thought of a serious illness terrified her. She couldn't imagine life without Megan. Without Megan's unconditional love.

"No, dear." Her mother tried to smile, rubbing the back of Ellie's hand. "I'm healthy as a horse."

"Thank God." Ellie's relieved grin was wobbly. Her mother was acting so oddly, Ellie hardly recognized her. Come to think of it, Megan wasn't even dressed for the office. She was wearing a casual pair of slacks and silk blouse, the kind of outfit she usually donned at home in the evening.

"Ellie, I'm ashamed to admit that I've done some pretty foolish things in my life." Megan glanced at the stranger again, met his gaze and held it.

Feeling suddenly left out, threatened, Ellie said, "Don't we all?" Though truth be told, she couldn't imagine her mother ever doing anything foolish. Megan was as savvy as she was big hearted.

Shaking her head, Megan smiled, though her usually sparkling blue eyes still had that stunned, almost unfocused look.

"I had a baby," Megan whispered, her gaze locking once again with the stranger's. The wistful, adoring look in her mother's eyes did nothing to dispel Ellie's confusion. Or worry. She was afraid to turn around, to see what kind of answering expression she'd find on the stranger's face.

"I know, Mom," she said gently instead. "You had five of them."

"No." Megan slowly shook her head. "I had six."

## CHAPTER SIX

"YOU LOST A BABY?" Ellie asked, stunned. Surely this was something they'd all have heard about. "When?"

"I was seventeen, Ellie—"

"Before Daddy?" Ellie felt a bit light-headed herself. As though she were watching the whole thing from far off and listening to her mother through a tunnel. It was too unreal.

Megan nodded again, turning her full attention to her daughter. "Before your father," she confirmed. "It was the summer after I graduated from high school."

Megan's eyes still had that faraway look, and Ellie knew that her mother had slipped into a place she couldn't follow. She could only sit there, shocked, and listen to the unbelievable story as it poured out.

"I was seventeen. The baby's father was twenty-one." Megan paused again, obviously remembering.

*Seventeen. And pregnant?* Ellie couldn't believe it. "What happened to him?" she asked.

"He made a lot of promises and then deserted me. My father later told me that he was killed in a freak riding accident."

Ellie's heart started to break for the young pregnant girl her mother had been. How dare anyone treat such a wonderful woman so carelessly! Squeezing her mother's hand, she sat silently at her feet, waiting for Megan to continue.

"My father wasn't pleased about the pregnancy, of course. He was afraid for my future. But when I insisted on keeping the baby, raising it alone, he supported my decision."

The stranger shifted behind Ellie. She'd forgotten he was there. She wondered, with another stab of fear, what any of this had to do with him. Blackmail maybe?

Megan kept her gaze trained on Ellie, though Ellie didn't think her mother was really seeing her.

"The baby was stillborn," she said, her voice filled with the tears she was trying so valiantly not to shed. "Or so my father told me."

"It wasn't?" Ellie asked, tensing.

Finally looking over Ellie's shoulder to the stranger, Megan shook her head. "But I didn't know that until tonight."

Megan's voice caught as the tears broke free and trailed slowly down her cheeks. She stood, walked over to the stranger, grabbed his hand and pulled him to her side. "He's your oldest brother, Ellie. Connor O'Hara."

"No!"

Ellie stared at the other man, trying desperately to take it all in. Oddly enough, the only coherent thought she could come up with was that she wished his eyes were a little warmer, filled with something…more…she didn't know what, just something more.

He smiled at her and his voice was gentle enough as he said, "Hello, again, Ellie. It's good to meet one of my youngest siblings."

"I don't believe this!" Ellie cried, staring at him. And then something registered. Her gaze pinned her mother. "You said he was Connor O'Hara."

Megan nodded.

"Connor O'Hara is our cousin. He's Aunt Clarise's son. We haven't seen him since the rift between her husband and Daddy after Grandpa died."

Still looking stupefied herself, Megan nodded again. "I know. That's what I thought, what we all thought—including your father."

Ellie noticed that her mother continued to cling to the man—her brother?—as she spoke. Megan wasn't really leaning on him, just holding him.

The man spoke again. "It's what I thought, too, Ellie. All the time I was growing up, in fact."

"You aren't Clarise's son?"

He shook his head.

"Clarise couldn't have children." Megan took up the story again. "Her father, your paternal grandfather, Harland Maitland, told her he'd arranged for an adoption for her and her husband, Jack. What nobody knew was that he'd arranged it with my father. The son they adopted was mine."

Ellie's gaze flew back and forth between the stranger and her mother. "Your father *sold* your baby and told you he was *dead*?"

Fresh tears spilled from Megan's eyes, but she stood tall as she nodded. "Pretty incredible, isn't it?"

"Too incredible," Ellie said. Nothing was making any sense. Nothing. All her life she'd heard nothing but good of both of her grandfathers. They'd been revered by the entire family, even those who had never had the chance to know them. "How do we know this is true?" she demanded. "How can we be sure he's not just some money-hungry grub after our fortune?" It wasn't as if it was the first time. And with all the recent publicity about the baby they'd taken in, some sick inventive soul might have gotten ideas…

"The letter proves everything," Megan said, handing Ellie the piece of paper from the top of her desk. "It's from Harland. I recognize his handwriting."

In her grandfather's distinctive penmanship, which Ellie recognized from documents she'd seen at home over the years, letters she'd pored over as a teenager trying to get a feel for who she really was, the family she'd been born into, she found the confirmation of Megan's incredible tale.

But Harland had been dead since the late fifties. The baby would only have been three years old. "Why is this coming out now?" Ellie asked, focusing on the practical—the only thing she knew how to do.

"Harland Maitland left the letter as a deathbed confession," Connor explained. "It was meant to go to Clarise, but Jack O'Hara intercepted it. He knew that it would break Clarise's heart if she found out what her father had done to Megan. And even worse Clarise would never recover if she lost her son—me—after having raised me as her own for three years."

Ellie stared at the man purporting to be her eldest brother. Part of her wanted so badly to believe him, if only for her mother's sake. For Megan having her long-dead firstborn suddenly come to life was a gift.

"Jack knew he had to estrange himself from the family so that the truth would stay hidden. That's when he caused the rift with your father, Clarise's brother—a nasty fight over financial matters pertaining to Harland's will. Having to choose between her husband and her brother, naturally Clarise chose Jack. They left town, and Jack forbade Clarise to have any further communication with the Maitland branch of her family."

Connor sounded pretty convincing as he related the facts. Ellie slumped on the couch at the far end of

Megan's office. She was exhausted. She still couldn't quite believe the man standing before her was actually related to her.

"Connor never even knew he was related to the Maitlands while he was growing up," Megan said.

Glancing between her two children, she finally left Connor's side, but Ellie could tell it was with difficulty. Megan settled herself in an armchair halfway between the two of them.

"My father, Jack, died when I was sixteen," Connor continued. The man was a good storyteller, and Ellie, engrossed, couldn't help but hang on his every word. "When she was going through his things, my mother—" he paused, seemed to catch himself "—my *adoptive* mother, found Harland's letter. Having just lost her beloved husband, she couldn't bear to lose her son, too, and vowed to take the truth to her grave, as her husband and father had before her."

While Megan lived all those years pining. What an amazingly selfish bunch. Ellie couldn't help the thought. Couldn't help being a little less proud of the family she'd been born into.

"But she knew I deserved the truth of my parentage," Connor continued. "So she wrote a letter and gave it to her attorney with the instruction that I was to receive it after her death."

"Clarise is dead?" Megan gasped.

Ellie was surprised to see the distress on her mother's face after all the woman had done to her. And yet, knowing her mother, she wouldn't have expected any less.

Connor nodded. "She died about ten months ago, but I was too confused myself to come right away."

Perhaps it was the fact that he'd had more time to get

used to everything that made Connor appear so calm, almost unaffected by it all.

"Did you have other family around you at the time?" Megan asked, her question filled with motherly concern.

Connor still standing where Megan left him, shook his head. "There's no one left but a few of my father's elderly relatives. I barely know them." He shifted his weight, looking uncomfortable. "My girlfriend was there, though," he said.

It sounded a little odd for a man of forty-five to refer to a woman as his girlfriend. And yet, it was also endearing. He seemed almost embarrassed by the admission.

"You aren't married?" Megan jumped on that one. Ellie was more than a little curious about his life, as well.

Connor shook his head. "Never have been. I'm a rancher—or was." He shifted awkwardly again. "Shortly after my mother, uh, Clarise died, Janelle left me, too."

"No!" Megan's heart was in her eyes as she watched her son. "Why?"

Connor shrugged, then looked away. "She says I'm a workaholic—that I love my ranch more than her."

For the first time, Ellie found something Maitland about the man. Or rather, something *Megan* about him. His work ethic. He'd fit right in with her other three workaholic brothers. Especially R.J.

Thinking of her eldest brother—second eldest now, she amended—Ellie wondered how he was going to react to Connor's sudden appearance. R.J. and his sister, Anna, had been adopted by Ellie's parents after their own mother died and their father deserted them. Robert, their father, was William's ne'er-do-well younger brother, and though Megan was really the children's aunt, Ellie knew that her mother loved R.J. and Anna as if they'd been hers from birth.

R.J. took his responsibilities as head of the family very seriously. Ellie hoped he wouldn't feel usurped by Connor.

Megan was asking Connor some questions about Clarise, the aunt Ellie had never met, and she found herself sympathizing with the other woman in spite of what she'd done. Megan believed, as did Connor, that had Clarise been told upon her father's death of Connor's true parentage, she would most certainly have given the child back to Megan.

Clarise had been a devoted mother and wife. She'd been loyal. She'd loved T-bone steak, which, when Connor mentioned it, made Megan smile. She remembered that about Clarise, as well.

"So you have a ranch in Amarillo?" Megan asked.

Connor shook his head, steady now as he faced Megan. "After everything happened, I ran into a bit of business trouble and had to sell the ranch. The truth was a bit shocking, you know?" he said, eyes only for Megan.

Nodding with compassion, Megan rose again and went to Connor. She drew him over to sit with her and Ellie on the couch.

"I've just been drifting kind of aimlessly the last few months," he said, almost as if speaking to himself. "I guess finding the way to come here."

"Or waiting until you were ready," Megan said softly. "I can't believe you're my son." She seemed to exhale the sentence, and started to cry once more.

Oddly enough, Ellie was the one who reached over and hugged her mother, comforting her. She understood

Megan's conflicting emotions—the incredible joy and desperate sorrow she must feel. To have missed almost half a century of her child's life… For someone like Megan Maitland, who'd dedicated her entire life to babies—her own and others—the blow had to be crushing.

And yet, Connor's presence was also a miracle.

"I'm going to ask you two to be quiet about this until I figure out how I'm going to tell the others," Megan finally said, taking one of their hands in each of her own.

Incapable of speech, Ellie merely nodded.

"Yes, ma'am," Connor said.

"What will we tell them now?" Ellie finally asked after several minutes had past.

Megan frowned, deliberated another moment. "I guess I'll have to introduce him as your cousin," she said. "That's who they'll think he is, anyway. I'll call a family meeting for tomorrow night."

Ellie nodded, relieved with the plan. Sitting in the living room at Maitland Mansion with her siblings, she was certain all of this would feel more manageable. "You going to invite the Lords, too?" she asked. Their friends would have to meet Connor soon, anyway.

Megan shook her head. "Let's just take this a little bit at a time, shall we?" Her eyes were shadowed again, and Ellie was willing to agree to anything to relieve her mother's suffering.

"In the meantime, I'll put Connor up in one of the family's condos—they're just a few blocks from here," Megan continued, her back straightening as she took charge. "And first thing tomorrow, I'll set up a bank account for you to see you through until you can get your affairs in order."

Alarm bells shot off in Ellie's head, but she held her tongue. There was enough money to share a little with Connor, and if he did turn out to be an impostor, her siblings would figure it out soon enough.

And if Connor were her brother—and Ellie didn't have any reason to believe he wasn't—he deserved all that Megan was offering him, and more. Ellie would never forgive herself if she hindered his acceptance by the family in any way.

Reaching across her mother, she clasped Connor's hand. "Welcome to the family, big brother," she said.

If he'd shown any outward emotion, she might have cried. For once, Ellie was glad her brothers weren't the demonstrative sort.

"I missed dinner," Megan said suddenly. "You two kids want to take an old lady out for a bite to eat?"

"You're not an old lady." Ellie jabbed her mother in the ribs with her elbow.

"I'm game for dinner," Connor said, pulling on the waistband of his slacks as he stood up.

Megan rose as well. "Ellie?"

Shaking her head, Ellie declined. She needed a break, time to assimilate all that she'd learned tonight. "I've got a few more things to take care of here…"

"You're going to find that Ellie'll give you a run for your money when it comes to being a workaholic," Megan said, smiling at her daughter.

Connor reached around his mother, giving Ellie a light punch on the arm. "Just make sure you don't work too hard, sis. You don't want to end up with nothing, like me."

Ellie joked with Connor as they made their back down the hall to her office. And she watched as Connor and Megan left her to head out to dinner. They were walking arm in arm.

Ellie couldn't find one thing about the man that resembled her mother. Except maybe his height. They were both tall.

And so were half a million other people in Austin.

DREADING BEDTIME almost as much as he dreaded mealtime, Sloan let the girls play with their blocks a little longer than he should have. They were going to be overtired and even more difficult to get down than usual, but he didn't have the heart to start a battle when they were playing happily.

He wasn't a fool.

Lying there on the floor a few feet away from them, taking the occasional bonk on the head when one of them tossed a block his way, Sloan wondered what Ellie was doing. A yellow square sailed his way and missed his nose by an inch. It wouldn't have mattered. Peace was worth a little pain.

Just as he was gathering up the motivation to insist on bath and bedtime, Sloan was saved by the ringing of the telephone. Grasping at any excuse to forestall the guilt he felt for keeping his girls up too late, he jumped for it.

"Sloan?"

Heart skidding to a halt, and then working double time, Sloan recognized Ellie's voice. "Yeah, Ellie, what's up?" *Please don't be calling to tell me the weekend was too much for you. That you've had enough.*

"I'm just finishing up here at the clinic and wondered if you were busy."

Her voice sounded odd.

"Not at all," he said, gauging how many hours it was

going to take him to get the girls to sleep. Now that they could crawl out of their cribs, getting them to stay there long enough to drop off was a real challenge.

"I know I'm being impossibly rude, but would you mind if I drove out for an hour or so?"

Frowning, Sloan told his heart to calm down. Despite the fantasies he'd been fighting about just such a request from her, something wasn't right. "Are you okay?" he asked. "You need me to drive in to the city?"

He'd have a better shot at getting the twins to sleep strapped in their car seats. Of course, they'd cry like hell when he tried to take them out again because that always woke them up.

"No, you've got the girls in bed, don't you?"

It was only seven-thirty, half an hour past their bedtime. "Almost," he said, stretching the truth just a little.

"I'd really welcome the drive, if you don't mind my coming."

"Of course, I don't mind," Sloan told her. "You sure you're okay?"

"Yeah—"

She didn't sound as if she meant it.

"—I just had something weird happen and kind of wanted to run it by you."

His heart started a thunderous rap again. And not because of any stupid sexual fantasies. Ellie needed him.

"I'll turn the light on," he said, then rattled off directions to the ranch before she could change her mind.

"Thanks. I owe you one."

Sloan would have laughed if she hadn't already rung off. She must really be unsettled to think that. He was so far in her debt, a hundred nights of coming to her rescue wouldn't catch him up.

Especially since coming to her rescue wasn't a withdrawal from his account—wasn't any kind of payment to her at all. No, fool that he was, he felt he owed her for that, too. It made him feel so damn good.

With more cheer than he'd been able to muster in a long time, he tackled both girls at once, catching one under each arm, and headed off down the hall with his screaming and kicking bundles.

Piece of cake. At least while he was stronger than they were.

THE DRIVE DID ELLIE GOOD. She had a theory that Texas open roads could cure just about anything. The openness, the vastness were just plain good for the soul. They put things in perspective.

But as she neared Sloan's turn off, she wasn't feeling any better about the evening's events. All the time Connor had told his story, he had never once shown any deep emotion. Not grief when he'd spoken about the deaths of the parents who'd raised him. Nor any particular joy to be reunited, after forty-five years, with his birth mother. Reticence was one thing. Ellie was used to that. But even with R.J., even when he was closing himself off from all of them, she could still *feel* him there. She'd felt nothing with Connor. As if he were made of stone.

And not just on the outside.

Driving through the gate at Sloan's ranch, Ellie wished that it were still light enough for her to get a good look at things. From the upright fence posts and the well-kept buildings she saw, it appeared Sloan had become quite successful. The spread was impressive.

He'd obviously been waiting for her. The front door opened before she even made it to the porch.

"Watch your step there with those heels," he said as she came up the slatted porch steps.

"As late as it was, I didn't want to take the time to go home and change," she said. She felt a bit more self-conscious about her looks than usual around him, dressed as she was in her gray suit, with its day's worth of wrinkles.

"I think you look great." He closed the front door behind her. "Very professional."

Ellie laughed. Professional she might believe—if she stretched it a little bit, given that she hadn't combed her hair since six o'clock that morning. But impressive? She didn't think so.

"You have dinner yet?" Sloan asked.

When Ellie admitted that she hadn't, he ushered her out to the kitchen and sat her at a wooden table large enough to seat a family of ten. She barely caught a glimpse of the living room as they passed, but it was enough to know that he hadn't taught his kids to help pick up their toys before they went to bed.

Sloan had just placed a plate of leftover casserole in front of her, when Ellie heard the telltale patter of little feet coming down the hallway beside her.

"Ariel, get back to bed right now," Sloan said. He tossed the towel he'd been using to dry his hands onto the counter and went after the little girl.

She sidestepped him, but lost her balance and fell. "Dwink," she said before he had a chance to scoop her up.

"Not until you get back in bed, young lady," Sloan said.

She started to kick the minute he had her in his arms.

Then she noticed Ellie. "Dwink," she cried, her little chin quivering as she looked at Ellie.

Before Ellie could say a word, Sloan said, "All right, but if I get you a drink, you promise to go right back to bed?"

Ariel nodded, her big brown eyes wide and innocent.

Ellie decided that it was just about time to give Sloan that list she'd promised him, before it got so long that it was running off the page. Meanwhile, she applied herself to her casserole. It might be a long night.

"This is really good!" she said upon his return. "Did you make it?"

Sloan shook his head. "My housekeeper, Charlie, does all the cooking."

She'd have asked about Charlie, except that there was a *clunk* from the other room. Whether it was Ariel again, or Alisha it was irrelevant. And not really a surprise, either.

Sloan appeared to be waiting until the child made her appearance. Or maybe he was hoping she might change her mind and climb back into her crib, where she belonged. Ellie figured there was a better chance of the sun shining in the window in the next five minutes.

"Do they do this all the time?" she asked him, finishing the last bite on her plate.

"Ever since they learned to climb out of their cribs." Sloan leaned his backside against the kitchen counter, watching her. "It's just a stage they're going through. They'll outgrow it."

Holding her tongue on that one, Ellie took her plate to the sink and rinsed it.

There was another *thump* from the other room— plastic toys spilling onto the floor, by the sound of things—accompanied by babyish chatter. Two voices of babyish garble.

"Mind if I put them back to bed?" Ellie dried her hands on the same towel Sloan had used earlier, trying not to find anything intimate in that action.

"Be my guest," he said, right behind her as she headed down the hall toward the sound of happy babbling.

Ellie would like to be his guest—permanently, she thought. In the great big unmade bed she passed on the way to his daughters' room. More conscious than ever of the weight of her unwanted virginity, Ellie wondered if maybe she should just do something to rid herself of that particular albatross. Especially after finding out that her mother had been sexually mature at seventeen. While Megan's ensuing heartache made it very clear that seventeen was too young, surely twenty-five was teetering on too old.

If Ellie could run an entire clinic, she could certainly take control of her sex life, too.

It was time.

## CHAPTER SEVEN

ARIEL AND ALISHA'S slobbery baby grins greeted Ellie as she appeared in the nursery. They were both dressed in pajamas with feet, sitting in the middle of the floor, attempting to stack square plastic blocks on top of a baby doll's belly.

"Dwink," Alisha said, scrambling to her feet. She toddled over to Sloan and held up her arms.

"Bed," Ellie said, intercepting the child. "You guys have had drinks, you've had playtime, and now it's time for sleeping." She carried the child over to the crib and put her in.

Before she laid Alisha down, Ellie looked around. "Where's the other crib?" she asked.

"Next door." Sloan stood, hands in pockets, in the doorway.

"Why?"

"That's actually Ariel's bed," he explained. "Alisha's is in her room next door."

"They have separate rooms?" That list was getting longer.

"Of course. I didn't want one to wake up the other if they ever cried in the night."

"What about keeping each other company?" Ellie asked. Picking Alisha up out of the crib and holding her on her hip, she moved purposefully into the other room. In Alisha's crib there was a blanket identical to

Ariel's, and a teddy bear lying on the mattress forlorn and forgotten. Ellie snagged them both up, gave the baby her teddy bear to hold, and made her way back to Ariel's room. There she deposited Alisha at one end of her sister's crib. She laid the baby down on her stomach, tucking the teddy in next to her, and covered her with her blanket.

Ariel was next. "Come on, punkin', you must be tired," she murmured softly, then kissed the baby's forehead and laid her down at the other end of her crib. "Alisha's right there by you. Now you lie down here and go to sleep." Carefully she tucked Ariel's blanket around her.

Both girls lay still for a second, as though waiting to see what happened next, and then both started to get up.

"No, darlings," Ellie said gently but firmly, rubbing them on their backs. "It's sleep time. You're right here together, now sleep."

Sloan watched the entire episode silently from the door. He knew what she was doing wasn't going to work, but he had asked for her help, and he'd let her give it a try before they both put their heads together and figured out what to do about his uncooperative children.

Thinking of the children would keep his mind off what he'd really like to do with Ellie. Things he'd really like to do, period. He was just that kind of guy.

His attention was drawn mercifully back to the crib as Ellie turned away several minutes later. But not, however, to admit the defeat he'd been anticipating.

The girls were sound asleep.

Sloan wondered why he didn't just give up. Apparently he was the only human being on earth incapable of managing his baby girls.

"SO THE TRICK is to let them sleep together?" Sloan asked as he poured a cup of coffee for Ellie and sat down opposite her at the kitchen table, his own cup between his hands.

His choice of room—the kitchen with a table between them—was probably good, she thought. Her decision to take control of her sex life had nothing to do with Sloan. She'd already offered her virginity to him. He hadn't wanted it.

She wasn't fool enough to offer twice.

"Sleeping together isn't the only thing," she said, forcing herself to concentrate on his words rather than on the way his hands were working his coffee cup. "You have to be firm with them, maybe rub their backs to help them settle down if they need that. But being together is important. They're twins, Sloan."

"Which is why I try to separate them when I can."

His brown eyes were so earnest. The man was really trying.

"I can't do that a whole lot in my current situation, but the one thing I made up my mind to do the moment we knew we were having twins was to preserve their individual identities. I want them to grow up independent and happy."

"And you naturally assumed that the two went hand in hand?"

"Of course," he said. He was so gorgeous from the waist up that it almost made her eyes water. Not that he wasn't perfect in every way from the waist down, but she couldn't see what was under the table.

"Like I said, they're twins. That doesn't just mean they look alike, that they share a birthday. It goes much deeper than that."

He was listening. Intently.

"This might sound odd, especially to a man, but twins share a peculiar, almost spiritual bond. A connection that exists without words. If they're going to grow up happy—and yes, independent—that bond must be tended to. Separating them is unnatural. It unsettles them."

"You're sure about that."

Shrugging, Ellie dropped her gaze from his searching eyes, afraid they might see more than he was looking for. "I can't be sure, no, not for everyone, but it's always been that way for Beth and me."

"Surely you two didn't share a room in that huge mansion!"

"Yeah, we did," Ellie admitted, looking back up at him. Her coffee was getting cold. "We shared a room until we were fourteen, and then, when we both had a need to claim space of our own, we ended up right next door to each other—with a connecting door between our rooms." She smiled self-consciously. "It's still there."

"The door?" He was leaning forward, and his smile captivated her.

"Yep. And though we keep it closed most of the time now, it's never locked." She'd never talked about this with anyone before—not even Beth. It was something they both had just seemed to know and accept. "We're both so busy with our separate lives that I hardly see Beth these days, but the bond is still there, part of who we are."

"I'll move them into a bigger room—together—tomorrow."

He was touching her with his smile. Ellie touched him back.

She had to stop.

"Putting them together at night isn't going to solve all of your problems with them."

"It's not?"

"No."

"Do you know what will?"

His corduroy shirt was rust-colored and brought out amber highlights in his dark hair. She mentally shook herself. "You sure you want to know?"

"Positive."

Because he sounded so determined, Ellie was completely open with him. "You need to change the way you parent."

"Obviously. But how?"

"Even though they're so young, you have to start setting limits."

He glanced down at the table and then back up again. "I do some of the time." His coffee was getting cold, too.

"More important, you have to stick to them."

Ellie's heart went out to him as he sat there silently. He really wanted to be a good father. "Children test their limits all the time, Sloan. It's natural, but part of their reason for doing so is to help them establish their world, to know what they can count on. Limits give them security."

Brows raised, he continued to listen.

"If they aren't given limits, they make their own."

"I can see that." A quick grin flashed across his face before he looked serious again.

"Yeah, but think about it. How can an eighteen-month-old baby possibly know what limits to set for herself? Because she knows so little about the world, she can't possibly know what's good for her."

Sloan nodded, and she could see that what she was saying was making sense to him.

"Take candy, for instance," Ellie continued, warming to her subject. She was thrilled, though not really all that surprised, now that she thought about it, that he was so receptive. "If given enough chocolate, a baby will eat until she gets diarrhea, throws up, or both. And why?"

"Because it tastes good and she hasn't been taught yet to fight temptation?"

Ellie smiled. He was starting to get the hang of it already.

"No, that would be when she's three or four and knows there's a *reason* to fight—or give in to—temptation. At this age, it's because she has no way of knowing that eating all of that candy is going to make her sick."

She saw light dawn.

"I get it."

"I knew you would."

Sloan leaned forward, the smell of his aftershave teasing her.

"Okay," he said. "Starting tomorrow, Ariel and Alisha won't know what's hit them."

His hand lay on the table between them, and she fought the urge to cover his hand with her own. "It might not be easy at first, you know," Ellie felt compelled to warn him. "It's going to take time, and a lot of consistency, to establish routines."

"They'll be testing me more than ever," he predicted.

"Right. But they'll feel more secure knowing you're in charge."

"I can handle it."

She didn't doubt that for a second.

THEIR COFFEE WAS COLD. Ellie excused herself to the bathroom, and Sloan figured he should probably clear away the cups before the stuff congealed right before their eyes, but he didn't dare. He was afraid that if they didn't have a reason to sit at the kitchen table, they'd end up in the living room. On the couch.

She was doing it to him all over again. There'd been a lot of girls in high school that Sloan had wanted. Truth be known, there were probably fewer that *hadn't* turned him on. But after listening to the guys talk, he'd thought Ellie would be one of those few.

He'd known Beth first. Gregarious and fun, she'd run with the popular crowd, always ready to try something new. During his senior year, Sloan had somehow ended up in the same crowd of kids. Probably because he'd had wheels. It certainly hadn't been because he was anything like them. He'd found their conversation rather meaningless.

And though they'd always been ready to go out, none of them had ever found much time for studying. Which was why Ellie never joined her twin. Beth was outgoing and sociable. Ellie studied all the time. The guys, in telling him about Ellie, said they guessed it was a blessing she was so smart. They made fun of her plain, practical clothes and old-lady hairstyle.

All their talk had lowered his guard. He'd been pole-axed that first time he'd met her, on a sunny fall afternoon when Beth had coerced Ellie into going with her to the mall after school. Beth hadn't been permitted to go unless Ellie was with her.

One look at Ellie and Sloan had seen the intelligence and hidden humor in her eyes. The rich chocolate color of her too-short hair. And unlike his less discerning pals, he'd seen immediately beyond the unattractive clothes to the slim shapely body they almost concealed. No one had told him Ellie was Beth's *identical* twin.

As soon as Ellie spoke to him that first day, Sloan couldn't make himself stay away from her. In Ellie he found a soul mate, someone whose thoughts went deeper than Friday night, who knew that life was much more serious than who had the coolest outfit.

He could, however, force himself not to touch her. By concentrating on the person she was every minute he was with her, by keeping his mind firmly on the challenge her conversation presented. By remembering his father. And his mother.

And by dating Marla more regularly. Marla, the girl from his side of the tracks who also ran with the rich kids. The girl he'd been sleeping with for more than a year...

"The house looks great," Ellie said, coming back into the kitchen. "Your housekeeper does a good job." Sloan was still sitting at the hardwood table, their cold coffee in front of him. They had more talking to do. They hadn't even gotten to whatever it was she'd needed to talk to him about. And they were going to do it right here—where he had one hundred pounds of solid cherry between his hands and her body.

"Yeah, Charlie's a good guy." Even if he was the most outspoken cuss he had ever met, Sloan thought. He could take anything Charlie had to dish out. His hide was thick.

"So what did *you* need to talk about?" Sloan asked.

Ellie almost blushed under that warm, compassionate stare. Even after all this time, the man was addictive.

*To every female who walked the earth,* she reminded herself. There hadn't been a single girl in her sophomore class who hadn't been in love with Sloan Cassidy. Except maybe Beth.

"Something happened at the clinic tonight, and I can't seem to step outside of it far enough to get a handle on it," she told him.

She'd actually forgotten for a little while about the evening's earlier events. The memories, as they returned, weren't any less disturbing the second time around.

"You have to promise me that you won't say a word to anyone about this."

Sloan nodded. "That goes without saying."

In his eyes she could see the trust she was looking for. "This man showed up at the clinic tonight…"

While Sloan listened attentively, she told him about Connor's arrival. About his claim that he was her long lost, supposedly dead eldest brother.

"Whew," Sloan whistled when she finished. "So you're certain the letter's legitimate?"

Ellie nodded, frowning. "That's just it, I *am* sure. So is my mother. Her son did not die as she was told. He was given to my aunt Clarise." She stopped. Looked at Sloan. "Clarise's letter confirms it."

"And this guy, Connor, he knew a lot of details about your aunt—things he'd only know if he'd been closely acquainted with her?"

"He knew that she always washed her hair with rose oil, that she took exactly twenty minutes in the shower every morning, that she had to have coffee before she put on her makeup each day. That she sometimes wandered the house in the middle of the night. My mom knew some of the same things about Clarise. Apparently the years hadn't changed her all that much."

"And they're things he could only have known if he'd lived with her."

"Yeah." Ellie nodded. "I must be crazy to think something's not right, huh?"

Sloan shook his head. He ran his fingers along the rim of his coffee cup. "Not crazy. Just cautious."

"You think I shouldn't be?" His opinion mattered. Mostly because Sloan had always been honest with her. Just as she'd been with him.

"Cautious is good."

"If he's my brother, shouldn't I be welcoming him with open arms?"

"Blood doesn't make family, Ellie. Love does."

Tears filled Ellie's eyes and she blinked them away. "My friend Lana said something similar the other day."

"Trust me, it's true." Sloan rose to dump their cold coffee down the drain. "My father's a perfect example of that. I have his blood, but we sure as hell have never been family."

Ellie was a little shocked by the vehemence she heard in Sloan's voice. Especially after all these years. She could understand when he'd been a child, still living in his father's house. But now...

"How'd your mother take the news?" Sloan leaned against the butcher-block counter by the sink.

Ellie thought about her mother. "Shocked, but really happy," she said. "You know, now that I know about her losing her newborn son, I'll bet finding little Cody abandoned last month was really hard on her."

"Probably."

"No one knew. She suffered in complete silence."

"Your mother's one classy lady," Sloan said. It made Ellie feel good to hear him say so.

"It's no wonder she was so adamant about taking him in." Ellie stopped as another thought occurred to her.

They needed to ask Connor if he might be the baby's father. Tomorrow night at the family meeting. Whether he was their cousin or their brother, he was a Maitland. And so, it seemed, was little Cody.

"How do you think the others are going to take the news?"

"Mom's not going to tell them yet—at least not all of it."

"Why not?" Sloan frowned, crossing one foot over the other.

"She said she needs some time to figure out *how* to tell them, which I can understand. I also suspect that she doesn't want any more negative publicity right now.

"She's going to introduce him as the man we thought he was—our estranged cousin. I don't know, maybe she thinks the others will take the news better after they've gotten to know him."

"There might be some merit in that."

Ellie thought so, too. After all, she probably wouldn't be feeling so uncomfortable about Connor now if she'd known him a little better before he'd been forced into her life.

They talked for another half-hour, Ellie sitting at the table and Sloan leaning against the counter. Then Ellie figured she'd best be getting back to the city. She had to work in the morning.

And if she sat there staring at the way Sloan's jeans molded to his masculine hips so superbly, she might forget her vow to refuse to fall for him all over again. She might have decided to lose her virginity—but not with him.

As they stepped outside, Sloan pulled the front door almost closed behind them. "I'll walk you out," he said.

It was dark enough out there that Ellie didn't argue. "Thanks for letting me come by," she said as they reached her Mercedes. Sloan held the door open for her, and Ellie stood beneath his arm, looking up at him.

"Don't thank me," Sloan said softly, dipping his head slightly as he ran one long finger along her lips. "I'm the one who owes you the debt of gratitude. You may have just saved my life."

She tried to smile, but her lips were quivering. "You'd have gotten it eventually."

"Maybe. But I doubt it."

"Well, glad I could help."

"Wait a minute," he said, just as she was getting ready to climb into the car.

"What?" She looked back at him. Did he want to kiss her as badly as she needed him to?

"You aren't done yet, are you?" he asked, looking worried. "Helping me, that is."

Knowing herself for the fool she was, Ellie shook her head as disappointment crashed through her. He didn't want her. He wanted her help. "Not if you don't want me to be."

"You think I'm ready to go it on my own?"

"No," she admitted, partly because it was true. And partly because, she was afraid. She couldn't bear to have him walk back out of her life. Not yet. "You've got some habits that are going to be hard to break. And handling two demanding babies alone is a difficult challenge for anyone. As a matter of fact," she said as another thought dawned on her, "that's probably what got you into trouble in the first place. You were overwhelmed and taking the path of least resistance just to stay afloat."

Lifting a hand to her hair and brushing it back from her brow, Sloan said softly, "Thank you for that."

"For what?"

"Finding a way to let me feel good about myself even when I'm a total failure."

She'd done that? "In the first place, you're not a failure—you love those girls, which is what matters in the end—and what I said is the truth."

Ellie waited, hoping he would keep touching her, that he would lower his head just an inch or two more and kiss her. Her entire body trembled as she anticipated the heat of his lips on hers.

Dropping his arm, he pulled the door open a little wider so that she could slip inside. His good-night was still ringing in her ears as she pulled out onto the main road.

And her body was still shaking.

# CHAPTER EIGHT

TUESDAY NIGHT, the entire Maitland clan assembled in the living room at Maitland Mansion. As always, Megan held court on the couch, Ellie and Beth on one side of her, Connor on the other. Everyone but Ellie was sending curious glances at the stranger.

R.J., silent and brooding, stood at the bar, a glass of whiskey in his hand. When the news finally came out, Ellie thought, it was going to be hardest on him. Anna and Mitch sat in armchairs, sipping glasses of wine. Ellie wasn't sure how they'd respond to their new brother. Only Abby was smiling, but then she was still too freshly in love to do much else. Megan was right to introduce Connor as their cousin at first. All of them, Ellie knew, would eventually welcome him with open arms. They were family. That's how they worked.

Ellie watched her siblings, feeling much more secure about Connor's appearance in their lives now that she was surrounded by them. Only Jake was missing. Oddly enough, her mostly absentee brother usually made Ellie feel safest of all. Closest to she and Beth in age, Jake had some mysterious job that kept him away from them much of the time, and Ellie missed him terribly.

"First of all, I want to thank everyone for coming on short notice," Megan began, making eye contact with each of her children. They all smiled back at her—even R.J. Of course they'd come when she'd called. They always did. And always would. Not because they'd been trained, or taught, or threatened to do so, but because every single one of them adored their mother.

Ellie waited, watching them all, especially R.J. She needed to know that her brother accepted Connor. R.J. was a great reader of people.

"I had a wonderful surprise last night and wanted to introduce him to you all as soon as possible," Megan continued. She took Connor's free hand. "This is my nephew, Connor O'Hara. Connor, your cousins."

A collective gasp followed Megan's announcement. Her children had all heard of the estranged branch of the family, of course, and of their cousin Connor. But none of them had expected to meet him. R.J.'s eyes narrowed. Mitch looked mildly curious. Anna and Abby stared. And Beth had her mouth open.

Megan gave them a few moments to recover from the bomb she'd just dropped, then proceeded to calmly make introductions. "R.J. is my oldest," she told Connor. "He's the president of Maitland Maternity."

Connor nodded at R.J.

"Anna's next," Megan said, "and aside from Jake, she's the only one who doesn't work directly for the family. She's a wedding consultant." Anna nodded at Connor, who nodded back.

Ellie wasn't sure, but she thought she saw a spark light in the man's eyes as they perused her eldest sister. She glanced at R.J. to see if he'd noticed anything, but her brother was re-filling his glass from the decanter beside him. For someone who didn't drink much, R.J. seemed to be downing a lot of whiskey lately.

Anna didn't appear upset by Connor's reaction, nor did anyone else seem to have noticed. Maybe Ellie needed to calm down—relax. She was letting this whole thing get to her, affect her good judgment. Was it because she knew Connor was really their brother? Did she have a selfish heart, after all, and not want to share her mother and her family any more? She sure hated to think she was that shallow, and vowed to make a special effort to ensure Connor's acceptance into their family was as happy, and painless, as possible.

Megan had introduced Mitch, Maitland's fertility specialist and Abby, the clinic's obstetrician.

"Ellie, you already know." With her new resolve, Ellie avoided the curious stares of her siblings and smiled warmly at Connor.

He smiled back.

"And next to her is her twin sister, Beth, who runs the day care at the clinic."

"Nice to meet you all," Connor said. He sounded as if he were there to do business with them. He'd certainly missed out on Megan's charm in his share of the gene pool.

"How'd you find us?"

"Does your family know you're here?"

"How long are you going to be in town?"

The questions flew, and Connor responded to them matter-of-factly, except for the ones Megan answered for him.

"Connor's ranch fell on hard times after his mother passed away," Megan explained. "I've put him up in one of our condos, and, this morning I set up a bank account for him until he can get back on his feet."

R.J.'s eyes narrowed again. He set down his whiskey glass. "Welcome to the family, Connor," was all he said.

"So, you fathered any children lately, Connor?" Abby piped up as silence finally fell around them.

Connor coughed. "Pardon me?" Rising, he went over to the bar and helped himself to another shot of whiskey from the bottle R.J. handed to him.

"She wanted to know if you could possibly have fathered any children lately," R.J. repeated. "Say, in the last ten months or so?"

Connor returned to his seat beside Megan. "You folks sure jump right into a guy's life, don't you?" he replied, easily enough.

"They have a reason for asking." Megan glanced at Ellie knowingly. "Is it possible?"

Shrugging, Connor looked around at all of them. "Sure, it's possible," he said.

He sounded a little egotistical to Ellie, like a guy who liked to kiss and tell. She mentally took herself down another peg or two. She wasn't going to be mean-spirited. She wasn't going to be jealous or selfish. There was enough of Megan to go around. With seven children already, what was one more?

"You said you'd broken up with your lady friend." Megan turned toward Connor. "How long ago was that?"

Looking down into his glass, he said, "Ten months ago."

"Do you think she could have been pregnant without telling you?"

Ellie noticed that her mother didn't even consider that Connor might have known the woman was pregnant, that he might have just plain deserted her. And Megan was generally an excellent judge of character.

"She wouldn't have done that to me," Connor said, encompassing them all in his glance. "She'd have told me."

"Can you be certain about that?" R.J.'s face was

drawn, tense. Maybe he just had a headache. He'd sure had enough to drink to earn himself one.

Connor didn't back down. "I know Janelle. She'd have told me."

Megan called an end to the meeting a short time later, telling her children that they could get to know Connor better at Thanksgiving dinner. For now, she wanted him to have some time to get acclimated without six inquisitive Maitlands climbing all over him.

Which meant Megan needed some time to get use to the situation herself, Ellie translated silently. Maybe spend some time alone with her newfound son. Funny, the thought of Megan needing time with Connor didn't leave Ellie feeling jealous or resentful. That was a good sign.

To her surprise, Connor was the first to leave. Ellie had expected him to hang around, spend some time with her mother—*his* mother. Of course, the events of the past twenty-four hours had probably taken their toll on him, as well. He must be exhausted.

"Obviously you're going to have him checked out," R.J. said the minute the door closed behind Connor.

"It wouldn't be smart not to." Mitch spoke as though it were a given.

Anna twirled her empty wineglass between her fingers. "Don't you guys think you should let Mom decide something like that?"

"No." Ellie hadn't meant to speak up. She glanced apologetically at her mother. "This concerns all of us."

Straightening at the bar, R.J. said, "I can have someone on it first thing in the morning."

*Whoops.* "I think we should let Mom do it," Ellie told her brother, thinking fast. "After all, this deals with

Dad's sister's family, and Mom's the only one who knew them."

"Are you all finished discussing me as if I weren't here?" Megan asked, her voice amused as she looked around fondly at her well—eaning but overprotective children.

"Sorry," five of them said at once.

Beth had been silent through the entire evening.

"I already intended to have his story checked out," Megan told them. "I might be a sentimental old fool, but I'm not stupid."

THE CONNECTING DOOR between Ellie's and Beth's rooms opened just as Ellie was climbing into bed that night. It had been a long time since that door had been used.

Still dressed in the stylishly casual capri pants and eyelet top she'd worn to the clinic that morning, Beth came in and sat on a corner of Ellie's bed. "So give me the scoop," she said, tugging at Ellie's toe. "You're so sly, knowing about this a whole day and not telling me."

"Mom made me promise." It was a half truth. Megan hadn't actually sworn Ellie to secrecy over their "cousin's" appearance. But as unsettled as she'd felt about Connor the night before, Ellie hadn't been able to speak with her twin about him. Beth would probably have picked up on her unease.

Her heart was still not welcoming the "too good-looking for his own good" rancher, but her head was working diligently to that end. And she felt a whole lot better now that everyone else had met him and Megan had agreed to have Connor's story verified.

"So what happened? How'd you get to meet him?"

Ellie related what she could of the surprise visit the evening before. She really hated not being able to tell Beth the entire truth.

Beth's gaze scrutinized her closely. "So tell me about the rest of the night. The part where you went out to Sloan Cassidy's and didn't get home until after I was asleep."

"There's nothing to tell." Trying to meet her sister's eye, Ellie succeeded in staring at Beth's top button. "I gave him a lesson in child care. And I left."

"He didn't try anything, did he?" Beth asked, her usual playfulness completely missing.

"No." Ellie wished like hell that she felt happier about that.

"Good." Grinning, Beth leaned forward. "I've got tickets to the new male burlesque in Dallas next week-end—" she said.

Sweet, funny, sexy Beth. She'd have the confidence to pull something like that off.

"—Mary Jane and Lana are coming. I bought a ticket for you, too."

Seeing the eagerness on Beth's face, Ellie almost wished she could go. "There's no way I can go to Dallas for the weekend," she told her sister. Unlike Beth's day care, Ellie's office was open seven days a week.

"It's on Saturday," Beth said. "Just fly up for the night."

With Sloan and his kids, she'd already taken on more than she had time for. Ellie shook her head. "I've got a test next week. I've got to study this weekend."

Beth hid her disappointment well, but Ellie sensed it anyway. "I'm sorry, Beth. You know I'd go if I could."

Beth nodded, bouncing the stuffed cat that usually sat

serenely at the end of Ellie's bed back and forth between her hands.

"So how's Brandon?" Ellie had only met Beth's new fiancé once.

"He's good. Just out of town again."

Ellie hoped her worries that the man wasn't being honest with Beth were unfounded. He seemed to be gone a lot. And always for different reasons. Work. A golf outing. Family reunions. A sick grandmother.

Beth wanted nothing more than to get married, have babies and raise them at her own day care. And Ellie had lost count of the times she'd heard Beth claim that she'd found the one man who could make those dreams come true.

Maybe she should ask Beth for one of her castoffs. If she put her quest to lose her virginity in her vivacious sister's hands, she could probably be done with it by nightfall the next day.

HE'D DIED AND GONE to heaven. Her body, naked before him, was more perfect than he'd imagined. Sloan's own naked body hardened immediately. She was standing a couple of feet away and was watching, a sexy smile on her beautiful mouth, as his shaft grew.

He stood there and let her watch.

And waited.

She'd come to him. And then his hands would finally know what his eyes had just discovered—the lusciousness of Ellie's curves. And the taste. He was going to taste every inch of her. Slowly. Insidiously.

With one step forward, she set him on fire. Then she took another step. He was an inferno. He was going to explode before he ever got to touch her.

She was perfect.

She was his.

Finally.

He tried to raise his arms, preparing to collect his bounty. And couldn't. They were tied. Big thick ropes strapped him in place.

Which made no sense. He was standing in the middle of his bedroom. What were the ropes tied to? And who would have tied them?

Ellie took another step forward, but somehow, between that step and the previous one, she'd put on his underwear. It was falling off her hips. He liked it there.

Lunging forward, he fought the ropes.

And woke up. His arms were tangled in the sheet that had been covering his body before he'd gone to sleep. His naked body.

Sweating, swearing, Sloan sat up. It was barely after midnight.

Damn. He was hot.

Climbing out of bed, he opened his bedroom window, allowing the October night air to soothe his aching body. He thought about putting on some underwear, maybe even pajamas if it would help tame him a bit, but he didn't move from the window. He was afraid to look at his underwear. To touch it. The image of it hanging off Ellie's body was too fresh to tempt fate.

"It's only because she's the last woman I've seen—the only woman I've spent time with recently," he told the night air. Though he felt a tad ridiculous speaking out loud to himself, he still felt better hearing the words. More in control. And it wasn't as if he wanted anybody to hear what he was saying. His problems were his own. He'd never spoken of them to anyone, and he damn sure wasn't going to start now.

"The dream wasn't about Ellie, it was about sex." He tried that one out. It felt good, too.

Leaning his hands on the windowsill, he stared up at the huge black Texas sky with its myriad twinkling stars. "It's just the same old thing," he told the man in the moon. "Me wanting sex. You've seen it a hundred times. Bet it's getting old, huh?"

The man didn't answer, but Sloan wasn't offended. He didn't need an answer. He knew all.

"Marla's been gone awhile now," he told the man, just in case the old guy had been too busy and missed that part. "She's the only woman I've ever slept with, and we both know I'm a man with a very healthy appetite."

It was probably just a cloud passing overhead, but Sloan could have sworn the man in the moon winked at him.

So now that they'd got the problem lying right out on the table—or the windowsill, as it were—what in hell was he going to do about it? His silent companion wasn't much help.

Gazing out at the vast land around him, the four thousand acres he'd created from dregs and turned into a successful Angus operation, he felt renewed. As if it were a whole new world stretching out before him.

Sexually speaking, too. He was no longer tied to one woman.

During his years with Marla he'd been faithful—sort of. Not that he hadn't been tempted. Lord—and the man—knew he had. A lot. More than any sane man could take. He'd been a little too close for comfort a couple of times.

There'd even been times, he was too ashamed to admit out loud, when he'd taken his wife, but in his mind he'd thought of another woman.

"So now that I'm no longer married, no longer tied to Marla in any way, I'm free to go out looking, right?" he asked the moon.

No answer. His body getting excited just at the thought, he took the man's response as a yes.

Feeling a little better, he pulled on the jeans he'd had on that day—minus underwear—and traipsed down the hall to the room his daughters now shared. As long as he was up, he might as well check on them.

They were doing fine, both sleeping soundly in their side-by-side cribs. Ariel's bottom was sticking up in the air. Sloan smiled. God, he loved them.

And that was why, he thought as his heart crashed, he *couldn't* go out looking. He couldn't do that to his girls. He'd die before he became the type of father his own had been.

Pulling Alisha's blanket over her shoulders, he headed dejectedly back down the hall to his room. With the window still open, he stripped down and lay back in the middle of his bed.

Once he gave in to his desires, he thought, they would control him, just as his father's had controlled him. They would drive away every other thought, every responsibility, until he was a slave to them, forsaking everything for the next lay.

Sloan never made it back to sleep that night. He was too afraid the dreams would return to haunt him. He'd rather be exhausted than hard.

He was up, shaved, showered, dressed and ready by the time his girls woke up.

"Your old man's sick and demented," he confessed to them as he entered their room. "But don't you worry, little ones, you won't ever have to pay for that. That I can promise you."

"Da-ee!" Ariel greeted him with her mostly tooth-less grin.

"Da-ee?" Alisha rolled over, saw him standing there, and stood up in her crib, reaching for him.

Grabbing a child in each arm, Sloan hugged them both tight.

A new day had begun.

A COUPLE OF THE RESPONSE CARDS for the invitations sent out for Maitland Maternity's twenty-fifth an-niversary gala the following March were waiting on Ellie's desk Wednesday morning. Both were sent with regrets.

Ordinarily, Ellie wouldn't have given the refusals a second thought. But with all the bad publicity the family was getting lately, she couldn't help but worry that the clinic's reputation was suffering and that people weren't coming to their party because they no longer wanted to be associated with the Maitlands. Deciding to wait until dinner to tell her mother about the returned invitations, she applied herself more vigorously to her work. Controlled what she could control.

The morning went well until she called the president of the Society for Maternity Care to speak about ar-rangements for the maternity health care and adoption convention that the clinic sponsored every year.

"I'm sorry, Ms. Maitland," Walton Smith drawled. "We always deal with *Mrs*. Maitland."

Ellie took a deep breath. She'd lost count of the number of times she'd come up against the same re-sponse over the past six months. In spite of working herself to the bone, regardless of the improvements she made at the clinic, she didn't seem to be gaining respect in the eyes of her accusers.

"My mother is no longer handling this part of our business, sir," she said. "She's devoting more of her time to a couple of the charities whose boards she sits on."

"I'm sure she'll change her mind when you tell her we asked for her specifically," Walton Smith persisted.

"There's no reason for that, sir." Ellie forced a calm she didn't feel into her voice. "I have the figures you need right here." Working with Drake Logan, Maitland Maternity's vice president of finance, Ellie had drawn up a budget to pay speaker fees for the upcoming convention, which would educate not only health care professionals, but also the public, on what could and should be expected for maternity health care in the twenty-first century.

"I'll take them from you, of course, Ms. Maitland," Walton Smith was saying, "but I'll need a call from your mother, verifying the amounts."

"I have the authority to give that verification." Ellie pretended she was a travel agent, talking someone into a trip to Hawaii. Anything to keep herself from hurling abuse at the man. Or bursting into tears.

Walton Smith finally took the figures from her and Ellie almost cried with relief.

"Thank you," he said, confirming the amounts one more time. "Now, you will have your mother call me, won't you?"

"Yes, sir." Ellie bowed her head.

"Today?"

The man had won. Couldn't he be satisfied with that?

"I'll give her the message right away," she said.

Hanging up the phone, Ellie wondered why she was killing herself if all she was going to be was a damn secretary.

"DID YOU HEAR?" Beth appeared in Ellie's office doorway late that afternoon.

Looking up from the papers in front of her, Ellie frowned. "Hear what?" she asked.

Even after a full day's work with demanding toddlers, Beth looked fresh, energetic. And as beautiful as always.

"That Markum bitch just put up a five-thousand-dollar reward if Cody's mother will come forward and name the Maitland who's the baby's father."

## CHAPTER NINE

"Damn."

For once, Beth didn't grin at Ellie's uncharacteristic use of profanity. As she walked into the office, she wasn't smiling at all. She plopped down in a leather armchair, hands gripping the arms as if she were ready to blast off.

"Can you believe that woman?" she asked. "Why won't she just go away and leave us alone?"

"Because we're rich," Ellie answered by rote.

"Because we have Cody?" Beth suggested.

Ellie grinned, getting into the game they'd been playing since they were kids. They'd lie on their beds in the room they shared and list their blessings. It had been Beth's way of dealing with the press, which was too often present in their lives.

"Because we're healthy and happy and own our own business, and she can't stand that."

"Her mother was mean, and she's mad she doesn't have ours," Beth said. Her sister always could come up with the best ones.

"I know," Ellie said, gaining momentum, "because she *wishes* she were as beautiful as you are."

Beth stopped, her arms dropping. "Why me?" she asked. "Why not 'us'? Have you looked in a mirror in the last twenty-five years? We're identical twins!"

A little shocked at her sister's outburst, Ellie wasn't

quite sure what to say. "We may have the same physical characteristics," she finally said, "but you package and carry them much differently than I do."

Beth's eyes softened. "Come out to dinner with us tonight, El," she pleaded. "Mary Jane and Lana are both meeting me here at six."

A night out under the scrutiny of her friends was not something Ellie relished, though she missed them a lot. She was going to have to find the time soon to at least have lunch with them.

"I can't, Beth," she said, unable to meet her sister's eyes. "I've got to get through all of this before I leave here tonight."

"I never see you anymore, unless it's at work," Beth complained, sounding disappointed.

"You were in my bedroom two nights ago."

Standing, Beth settled one thigh on the corner of Ellie's desk. "I'm worried about you," she said, suddenly serious. "It's not necessary, you know—all this time you're putting in here."

"I have a job to do."

"Yeah, *a* job. So why are you doing enough for two jobs?"

Ellie looked up and held Beth's gaze. "I have to do this, Beth. I have to know that I can, that Mom didn't just hire me because I'm a Maitland."

"Mom didn't."

"I don't know that," she whispered.

"Well, you should." Beth stood up straight. "El, you're trying so hard to prove yourself when you know, as we've always known, that the opinions that matter are those of our own family and close friends. They're the only ones we can trust. And all of us are already positive that you're the best person for the job."

Ellie smiled and got up to give her sister a hug. "Thanks," she said.

But she knew, watching her sister's back as it disappeared down the hallway, that for once Beth just didn't understand.

SLOAN HAD A HEADACHE. In body and in spirit. Head in his hands, elbows on his desk, he'd just about reached the end. Out weaning calves that afternoon, with Charlie listening in while the girls took their nap, he'd discovered that several of his best Angus were missing. And much of his southern fence line was down, too.

"Da-ee!" Alisha pulled herself up his desk chair, her little fingers stretching way above her head to the desktop. Sloan's hand barely caught the pile of bills he had yet to pay that evening before she'd swept them to the floor. She got an eraser instead, and plopped down on her padded fanny to investigate the new treasure.

Meanwhile, Ariel, on the other side of his desk, managed to get hold of something blue—the mini-planner he'd received free in the mail and was intending to dispose of. She could play with it, and nothing of value would be destroyed, he thought.

"I-keem!" Alisha said, dropping the eraser.

"I-keem!" Ariel echoed. She was sitting on the floor to one side of his desk, her back to him, chewing on the planner.

Sloan stood, on his way to do their bidding, when the phone rang.

"Cassidy," he answered brusquely, half his mind on the girls' antics. Alisha had picked the eraser back up and was trying to shove it between his desk and the wall.

"Sloan? It's Ellie."

*Thank God.* "Hey, El," he said, trying to infuse enough calm and good cheer into his voice to fool her. "How's it going?"

"Okay. Work's been better, but that's par for the course."

Looking around him, at the toys, scrap paper and what used to be magazines littering his office floor, Sloan could relate to that.

"Listen, I don't want to keep you," she said. "I just called to see how things were going."

He could lie.

"Terrible."

"What's wrong?" she asked, her voice suddenly full of concern. "Are the girls all right?"

Well, they weren't screaming for their ice cream. "For the moment."

"It's only been a couple of days, I told you it would take time."

"I know, and actually, there's been some improvement." He told her about getting them dressed that morning. He'd done it all before breakfast, and there hadn't been a single tear.

"Good for you!" she said, and then added, "So what's the problem?"

"I think they used up their quota of 'be good for Daddy'." With the day's paperwork still waiting for him, he didn't have the time to chat, he thought, but it felt so damn good to talk to Ellie.

"That's where the taking time part comes in. You're sticking to your guns, aren't you?"

Did "just barely" count? "So far."

"You don't sound too sure about that."

She'd already been such a help to him, he didn't want to burden her any further, and he didn't see what she could do to help him out of his current predicament, anyway. Not unless she had a cattle finder and thief apprehender sitting around in a desk drawer someplace.

"I've got a bit of a problem here at the ranch. It's taking extra time, and the girls aren't cooperating."

"What's wrong?"

"Someone's been stealing cattle right out from under my nose." He waylaid Ariel as she toddled past, and removed his checkbook from her fingers, replacing it with the plastic planner he'd thought she had. "About fifteen of my herd are missing. I've reported the theft to the Texas and Southwest Cattle Raisers' Association, and they're sending out an investigator. But in the meantime, I've got fence to repair."

"So what have you been doing with the girls up until now, when you've been working?"

Sloan rubbed the aching spot between his brows. He really had to start getting more sleep. "Charlie's sister was here for a while. Mostly, I've just taken one hell of a long vacation, but it's time to get back to work."

"So bring them here."

She made it sound so simple. "There?" She had as much work to do as he did. Did she really think the girls would sit on a blanket on her office floor and play quietly all day?

"Beth owns and runs the day care here at the clinic," Ellie said. "I'm sure she'd be happy to have them."

Day care. That wasn't what he wanted for his girls. He wanted them to be raised at home by their parents—*parent*. Not in an institution.

"Beth's great with the kids," Ellie said as he hesitated. It was almost as though she could read his mind. He wasn't sure she couldn't. He could hear Alisha grunting behind him as she tried to force the too-large eraser into a too-small crack.

"She's a certified preschool teacher, and both of the women she has working for her are certified, as well."

Ariel was tearing the pages out of the planner. "Are you sure she'd want them?" he asked.

"Of course. With kids and Beth, the more the merrier." Ellie chuckled. "I sometimes think it's because she never stopped being one herself."

He remembered Beth from high school. Fondly. "I can certainly understand how the kids would have a good time with her."

"It would be good for the girls, too, Sloan," Ellie said, her voice gentling. "They're kind of isolated out there on the ranch. Which is good for them in a lot of ways," she inserted in a hurry, "but this will give them a chance to play with other kids."

She had a point. A good one.

"Is tomorrow too soon to bring them?"

Ellie laughed. "I'll let Beth know they're coming."

LOUNGING IN A CHAIR on her private balcony, the phone beside her, Janelle frowned. And took another long drag on her cigarette. The room was Nonsmoking, but who the hell cared. What she took into her own body was nobody else's business.

What in the hell was taking Petey so long to call? They'd said one o'clock. It was now after two. Janelle didn't mind being a lady of leisure—especially not now that Petey had wired her some money and she could afford to leisure in a place like this. But she was worried. She needed to talk to the loser. He was all she had at the moment.

It was almost another hour before the phone rang.

"Finally. What took you so long?" she demanded as she picked up the receiver. The man really was much too stupid for her.

"I was out to lunch with Megan."

*Oh. Sure.* He got to hobnob with the rich and famous while she was sitting here by herself, bored.

"You think they bought your story?"

"I'm sure of it."

Another thing that got on her nerves about her worthless husband. He was always too sure about everything.

"There should have been something in the news about Lacy by now," she said, hoping to bring him down a peg or two. All he did was enjoy himself, while she did all the work. All the planning and worrying. Why should he get the easy out?

"You worry too much," he drawled. "More 'n likely, she was taken to the morgue with Jane Doe tagged to her toe. Jane Does ain't newsworthy."

"A dead woman found in the alley behind Maitland Maternity Clinic is what's newsworthy, you moron."

But what did he care? He wasn't the one who was going to take the rap for murder if something went wrong. Unless she could figure out a way for it to look as if Petey had been the one who...

Lighting another cigarette, her fifth in an hour, Janelle forced her mind back to the problem at hand. There'd be lots of time later to work out the logistics of another murder scenario.

Petey was busy telling her again that she worried too much.

"They'd have found her right about the time the baby appeared, Pete," she said derisively. "That would be suspicious enough to warrant an investigation of some kind." Anyone with a brain could have figured that out. But then, she'd figured out a long time ago that Petey didn't have a brain.

"Maybe someone found her before the authorities did," Petey said. "You know, someone who got some use out of that chic's body before dumping it somewhere else—far away from the clinic."

"Yeah, well, just in case, you keep your eyes and ears open for any sign of a blonde-haired, blue-eyed chic that would make you puke she's so goody-goody looking."

Slamming the phone down, Janelle got up to make herself beautiful. With her husband so wrapped up with the Maitlands, she suddenly had other needs on her mind.

Might as well make good use of the waiting part of this game, she thought, stripping on her way to the shower. Grinning, she watched herself in the mirror as she ran her tongue over her lips. And felt another satisfying flame of desire flare inside her.

THOUGH ELLIE HAD a quick bite to eat with Sloan and the girls Thursday night when he came into town to collect them from their first day with Beth, she didn't see him again all weekend. She hadn't been stretching the truth when she'd told Beth she had to study. She had her first exam coming up in an advanced business law course she was taking, and had some reading to catch up on.

Charlie's niece was down from Dallas for the weekend and had offered to watch the girls for Sloan on Saturday so that Sloan could finish repairing his south fence.

She didn't see him when he dropped the girls off

Monday morning, either. Midmorning, when she went to check if they were there, she did see Chelsea Markum hanging around. She managed to avoid the gossip-hungry shark—barely.

Connor wandered into her office shortly after lunch, and though she'd made it a goal to spend some time getting to know him, she had to brush him off. She had a meeting with Walton Smith to approve the list of speakers he intended to invite to the maternity care convention and to go over workshop topics. Though the clinic didn't host the convention, or have anything to do with the actual running of it, as a major financial sponsor, they did retain the right to oversee the content. He'd finally allowed Megan to convince him to work with Ellie on the project.

Ellie'd done her homework and was completely prepared. She had in front of her a list of the speakers of the previous three years, statistics on which workshops were well attended and which were not, a list of requested speakers for future conferences, as well as standard speaker fees. Already familiar with many of the big names in the industry, she felt ready to impress the pants off Walton Smith.

Ellie had just thrown away her stale tuna sandwich, her unfinished lunch, when he knocked on her door, a full fifteen minutes early for their appointment. If he'd hoped to catch her off guard, he'd be disappointed.

"Mr. Smith." She stood and shook his hand, then offered him the chair in front of her desk.

Looking around before he sat, the dapper little man seemed to take in everything from Ellie's business suit to the titles on her bookshelf.

"Ms. Maitland." He nodded to her as he sat, and Ellie couldn't be sure, but she thought she detected a new note of respect in his voice. "I've the list here for you to go over, feel free to add or change as you see fit."

At least the condescending tone was gone.

For the next half hour, Ellie forgot everything but the business at hand, working so well with Walton Smith that she almost forgot there'd been any animosity between them. They shared the same vision for the conference, the same mission. The planning part was almost fun.

"I'm not sure about Dr. Rosenthal," Walton said at one point. They'd moved over to the couch and coffee table across from her desk so they could both see the list they were creating. "His name comes up every year when we ask for suggestions for speakers, and yet no one I've spoken to has ever heard of him. He's in Europe someplace."

"I know of him," Ellie said. "My sister Abby took a seminar of his a couple of years ago. I'm sure she still has a pamphlet on him in her office downstairs. If you want to look through these—" Ellie handed him writeups about a couple of candidates she'd come up with on her own "—I'll go see if I can get something on Dr. Rosenthal, and be right back."

Ellie took the stairs down to the first floor, practically skipping as she went. Not only had she earned Walton Smith's respect, but she was actually enjoying herself. Something she hadn't done at work since the first rumor of nepotism had started to circulate.

Ellie waved at Hope Logan as she passed by the gift shop. Hope managed the gift shop for them and was like part of the family. She was married to Drake Logan, their vice president of finance, but the two had recently separated. Ellie reminded herself to stop in and see Hope soon.

Abby's office door was in sight, but the sound of sudden crying from the day care stopped Ellie in her tracks. She knew that cry—correct that—*those* cries. Something was wrong with the twins.

Ellie pulled open the center's glass door, her gaze immediately seeking the two towheaded babies she'd already begun to feel close to. One of them was crying simply for the sake of crying—she could tell that immediately. It was the other cry, the first one she'd heard, that alarmed her. The cry of pain was vastly different from one of temper or exhaustion.

Beth had Ariel on her lap, and was rocking the baby back and forth as she sobbed. Alisha stood next to Beth, balancing herself with both fists on the seat of Beth's chair. Lizzie and Cheryl, Beth's assistants, were seeing to the other children.

"What happened?" Ellie asked, reaching for Ariel first. She had to see how bad the damage was.

"E-wee." Alisha cried harder when she saw who'd taken her sister. "E-wee!"

Ariel burrowed into Ellie's chest, her little body shuddering with sobs.

Beth picked up Alisha, holding her close enough for one wet hand to grasp Ellie's silk jacket.

"She was trying to run after Ricky, and tripped and hit her chin on the floor. She hasn't let me look at it yet, but there's no blood," Beth reported, all business. Concern filled Beth's eyes, and Ellie knew how personally Beth took it when one of her little charges had an accident.

"Let Ellie take a look," Ellie said to Ariel, who just cuddled in tighter. "Ariel, come on, sweetie, Ellie needs to take a look."

Ellie had a seat and, repeating the words over and

over, finally managed to move the little girl's face away from her breast enough to get a look at her chin. "You're right, there's no blood," she reported to her sister, who was hovering over her, Alisha still in her arms. At least the other baby, secure now that Ellie was close by, had quieted.

"Yeah, but it's purpling up nicely," Beth said, examining the bruise for herself.

Ariel's tears had lessened, but the baby still hiccuped with sobs.

"She's going to be just fine," Ellie said, smiling at the little girl. "Just took a bump, that's all."

Ariel's thumb slipped into her mouth.

"I'm going to have someone in pediatrics look at her just the same."

Taking Alisha with her, Beth ran to find a pediatric nurse. Nervous now about leaving Walton Smith for so long, Ellie knew that she couldn't go anywhere until someone had had a look at Ariel. The baby would be scared to death to have a stranger, no matter how sweet and gentle, poking at her.

Fifteen minutes later, Ariel was pronounced fit as a fiddle, except for her colorful bruise, and Ellie flew back up the stairs to her appointment, an apology forming on her lips as she ran.

Walton Smith was waiting impatiently, briefcase in hand, when Ellie hurried into her office. The table where his papers had been spread was empty, and his bald head was practically shining with indignation. He glanced pointedly at his watch.

"I'm sorry," Ellie said, forcing herself not to pant. She hadn't had time to come up with a plausible excuse for a twenty minute absence without lying so she opted for the truth.

"A friend of mine has his babies downstairs in the day care, and one of them just took a tumble," she explained. They weren't through with their business yet. She had to convince the man to sit back down, and reestablish the rapport she'd worked so hard to attain.

"The child was seriously hurt?" Walton asked, his thin gray brows puckering with concern.

"No." Ellie smiled. "She bruised her chin, but didn't even break the skin. She just needed some coddling."

Smith moved toward the door. "You don't have staff downstairs to take care of that?" he asked.

"Yes, but—"

"Obviously you aren't yet mature enough or experienced enough to handle your responsibilities, Ms. Maitland. Or to ascertain just which ones are yours to handle. I've been waiting almost half an hour, and now I have another appointment that I must get to."

Ellie continued to apologize profusely, but the man would not be appeased. He left, saying he'd have his secretary fax over a final list of workshops and speakers. His tone left no doubt that Ellie would be expected to accept his final decision. She saw him to the elevator, still trying to make amends, and then went straight to her mother's office.

"I screwed up," she said, sitting primly on the edge of a seat in front of Megan's desk.

Dropping her pen, Megan folded her hands on the desk in front of her. "What happened?"

"I was having my meeting with Walton Smith, and it was going better than I ever dared hope…"

"He gave you the respect you deserve?"

Ellie nodded, wishing her mother could have been there, seen the good before she had to hear the bad. "More than that, he was asking my opinion. We were really working well together, creating a program that will probably be the best this conference has ever seen."

Megan smiled. "Go on."

Ellie told her mother about the trip downstairs for the pamphlet, her detour, and Walton Smith's subsequent reaction.

"That's unfortunate," Megan said, her tone solemn.

"I was wrong to keep him waiting, I know that," Ellie hurried on, barely hearing her mother. "And I'm sorry—"

"Ellie," Megan interrupted, leaning slightly forward. "You did nothing wrong." Megan's voice was gentle, but carried authority. "It was unfortunate that Mr. Smith had to wait, but unfortunate is all it was."

"But he was so angry..."

Shrugging, Megan smiled sadly. "Some people just don't understand priorities, honey. You had no way of knowing the child wasn't badly hurt until Pediatrics had had a look at her."

"He said that there were capable people downstairs to deal with the baby. That my job was upstairs and that I'm clearly not experienced enough to determine what is my responsibility and what is not."

"And Mr. Smith's simply not mature enough to determine what really matters." Megan's voice brooked no argument.

Ellie left her mother soon after, aware that as far as Megan was concerned the incident was over. Back in her own office, Ellie wasn't so sure. She was tired and achy from carrying too much weight on her shoulders. As hard as she tried, it was never hard enough. It seemed as though no matter what she did right, people were always out there waiting for her to fail. She couldn't shake thoughts of the very real possibility that her mother wasn't able to be objective in her case. That Megan had wanted Ellie in the family business so badly, she'd given her a job simply because of family connections—not because of Ellie's qualifications.

## CHAPTER TEN

ELLIE QUIT WORK EARLY. The walls didn't cave in as she locked her office door and walked down the hall. The carpet didn't curl up in shock. She felt too battered to give herself a hard time for leaving. Not wanting to stand around and wait for the elevator in case something called her back, she hurried down the stairs.

When she reached the first floor, she was struck with another idea—maybe one that had been germinating and just needed her to get out of her office before it took root. Slipping into a vacant office, she dialed the ranch.

Sloan answered on the first ring.

"I'm leaving early today. Can I save you the trip into town and bring the girls home?"

"Of course! That'd be great." Sloan's elated tone changed when he asked, "Is something wrong?"

"No," Ellie replied, forcing herself to sound cheerful. "Not at all." Not if you didn't count a body and soul that were just plain worn out from trying. "Well, Ariel has a purple chin, but Katie looked at it, and it's nothing to worry about."

"What'd she do?" he asked, as though a bruise was nothing new when it came to his girls.

"She was chasing boys and tripped."

Sloan groaned. "Tell me they don't start that young. It's not instinct yet, right?"

"No, Sloan." Ellie laughed for the first time in hours. "Ricky had a truck she wanted to play with."

"Oh." He was breathing easier. "Good. But what about car seats?"

"I'll borrow some from the day care." She'd already thought of that. "Beth keeps a couple for emergencies."

"Drive carefully" were Sloan's parting words before he rang off.

Words that left Ellie feeling warm all over.

THE GIRLS FELL ASLEEP in the back of her Mercedes the minute Ellie hit open road. As she drove out to the ranch, she started to relax and let the day roll over her. She didn't feel any better about what had happened. She had just quit worrying about it.

As the miles flew by, she found herself glancing back in the rearview mirror, checking on her charges. *Drive carefully,* Sloan had said. His voice had been caring, and she'd known what he'd meant. She was carrying everything that was dear to him in the backseat of her car. It made her feel good that he trusted her that much.

And a little sad that she hadn't been included in the thought. Or maybe more than a little sad. She'd give just about everything she had to have Sloan care for her that much.

Jerking her thoughts to a screeching halt, Ellie flipped on the radio, scanning for some news or something to concentrate on. She'd come into this situation with her eyes wide open. She wasn't going to let Sloan Cassidy break her heart a second time. He wanted a friend. Nothing more. And she had a job that required all her energy.

Alisha stirred, her little hand reaching out, only to

fall back against the bar of her car seat. Ellie turned off the radio. She hadn't meant to disturb them.

Another couple of miles, and Ellie glanced into the mirror again. The girls were so precious, their blond curly heads cranked over to rest along the sides of the car seats. One was in purple overalls, one in yellow, and they were both filthy, a testimony to the hard day of fun they'd had. Alisha's funny little curl was plastered down to her forehead.

Another quick peek assured Ellie that Ariel's chin was already looking better. She drew herself up short. She was acting as if the child were hers. Remembering when she'd first heard Ariel's cry that afternoon, and her immediate response, Ellie started to sweat. She had no business thinking of those girls as part of her life except on a very temporary basis. She had no claims to them.

Except that she did. She felt, in some small, danger-ous way, that they were a little bit hers.

"They aren't," she whispered. "They aren't mine," she repeated a little louder. But the increased volume didn't help; she wasn't convincing herself.

How could she, when holding them, being the one who could console them had felt so damn good?

One thing was for certain, Ellie told herself, chin in the air, as she took a final glance back, the feeling wasn't one-sided.

When Alisha had been frightened and upset that af-ternoon, she'd called Ellie's name.

SLOAN JUMPED in the shower. He figured he had about twenty minutes tops to get the day's sweat and grime off his body and find a clean pair of jeans to pull on. Given the dirt that was part of a cowboy's life, he was probably going to need every second of that time. He was being a fool, he knew, but he wanted to be clean-smelling and fresh for his girls. All three of them. Dinner was in the oven, and the evening ahead seemed just about as perfect as it could get.

Ellie obviously drove slower than he did. He was dressed and pacing the front porch by the time she arrived.

In record time the girls were strapped into their high chairs, baby plates of food suctioned to their trays, and for once, Sloan got to taste his food before it was cold. Used to allotting one arm per child, he didn't usually have a hand left over to feed himself. With Ellie there, taking on Alisha, he could tend to Ariel and eat, too. Life kept getting better and better.

"THERE'S BEEN A STRANGER around the past couple of weeks." Chelsea Markum popped her head into Ellie's office the next afternoon.

Wishing she'd shut the door, Ellie ignored the woman. She had a lot of work to get through before class—and her exam—that night.

"You wouldn't happen to know who he is, would you?"

She'd received a faxed spreadsheet with the list of speakers and the maternity conference workshop schedule from Walton Smith's office. Dr. Rosenthal wasn't there. But the rest of the program looked good.

"You don't need to tell me, of course." Chelsea left the doorway and approached Ellie's desk. Her height alone had once been enough to intimidate Ellie, let alone the fact that she was model gorgeous. But Ellie was immune to the auburn-haired reporter by now.

"I can always do my own checking…"

"He's my cousin, Connor O'Hara, from Amarillo."

"Clarise's son?" Chelsea's eyes widened.

Ellie nodded, still studying the spreadsheet in front of her. Or pretending to. She had to hand it to Chelsea: the woman did her homework. It suddenly became paramount that Chelsea be convinced Connor was who they said he was. She couldn't take a chance that the woman really would look as far back as Connor's birth, inadvertently discover her mother's illegitimate pregnancy and put two and two together. That would be devastating for her mother; Megan wanted to revel the truth to her family herself.

Chelsea would never be able to prove anything, of course. Not without the letter that her mother now had locked away in her safety deposit box.

But since when did Chelsea need proof to spread her innuendo and lies?

"I thought that branch of the family had nothing to do with you."

"They didn't, but Clarise died several months ago, and apparently whatever dispute separated the family died with her. Connor's all alone now, and came to find us."

Chelsea's green eyes narrowed. "He's the father."

Ellie could almost feel the other woman's excitement across the room.

"No," she stated unequivocally. "He's not."

"You're certain about that?"

The reporter clearly didn't believe her. "He didn't even know the baby existed until we told him."

Chelsea's face showed her disappointment. "He could be lying."

Ellie tensed. "He could be, but he's not." She met

Chelsea's challenging stare. "He was as shocked as we were, and absolutely certain the baby's not his."

"So what'd he show up for—money?" the reporter asked over her shoulder as she headed for the door.

Ellie didn't validate the question with a reply, but the woman's parting shot had hit its mark. She was scared to death that was exactly why Connor was here. And that her mother was going to be hurt beyond belief.


"WHOA, THERE, LITTLE GIRL." Sloan grabbed his daughter's slippery body with one hand, preventing her from sliding under the water.

During Thursday night's bath, Ariel showed her gratitude with a big splash, soaking Sloan, Ellie and her sister in the process. Alisha, screaming with delight, joined the fun.

With one hand on the little girl's thigh to hold her in place, Ellie leaned as far back as she could get, away from the spewing fountain.

And bumped shoulders with Sloan. Their glances met. Her laughter died on her lips.

The tile floor in the girls' bathroom felt like cotton beneath her knees, and the lukewarm water seemed to be giving off enough steam to make her sweat.

Sloan smiled at her. She smiled back.

Ellie had no idea how long they might have sat there, had Ariel not shrieked and flung water at her father, soaking the front of Sloan's shirt. Alisha, not to be left out, caught Ellie beneath the chin. Water trickled down her neck. But at least her silk blouse was spared.

She'd have been spared completely had she not been so foolishly preoccupied. She was up on the girls now. Could anticipate their moves most of the time. And one thing she knew was that Alisha always followed her twin.

Just as Ellie had always trailed in Beth's shadow.

"WHAT ARE WE DOING HERE?" Ellie asked Sloan that evening after the girls were in bed. They'd had a rough moment there in the bathroom. At least she had. And she had the distinct feeling that he had, too.

"I don't know." He didn't pretend ignorance. They were sharing a cup of coffee at his kitchen table before she headed back to the city. This was the third time she'd been able to bring the girls home for him, counting the night she'd left work early. The third night they'd shared dinner, bathtime and a bedtime story. The only night she hadn't been there that week was the night she'd taken her exam.

Studying him, Ellie couldn't help wishing, just for a second, that she was the type of woman that turned Sloan on. Really turned him on. Enough to spur him to make something more of the brief moments of awareness that seemed to be springing up between them.

Except that she didn't have time for the kind of love Sloan would inspire in her. She'd managed to do well on her exam this time, but…

She also didn't have time for the heartache that would follow when he couldn't return that love.

"I think we're building a friendship," Sloan finally said, meeting her gaze head-on. "A real one."

Which told her so much—and nothing at all. "Okay."

He was leaning slightly forward, damp shirtsleeves rolled up, forearms resting on the table. His hair, thick and dark, tumbled over his forehead. Ellie ached with desire.

"You're important to me, Ellie."

Her heart rate sped up.

"And I think what means the most is that the friendship is based on things that last, like respect, trust, shared values, stimulating conversation."

Kind of like her friendship with Lana, she thought. Or Mary Jane. Or her mother.

She nodded.

"If it were sexual, it would be temporary. This isn't."

How could she be so warmed and yet so hurt at the same time? He wanted to be her friend for the long term, in her life permanently. He just didn't want her sexually.

"Say something."

*What? That it's sexual for me? That my body's so on fire for you right this instant that I'm going to die if I don't feel you touch me?*

"I'm glad we're friends."

ELLIE HADN'T BEEN GONE long enough to make it back to the city when Sloan's phone rang.

"Cassidy," he said, his heart going into overtime as he pictured her stranded somewhere.

"Hi."

Dinner turned to lead in his stomach. "What do you want, Marla?"

"Oh, Sloanie, is that any way to talk to your wife?"

She'd dropped her voice to the babyish drawl that drove him insane.

"Ex-wife."

"The divorce was only for convenience, Sloan. It didn't mean anything."

Sloan's senses sharpened as he translated: Marla wanted something. He sank down onto the leather couch, his feet straight out in front of him, his head resting against the back of the couch.

"How's New York?'' he asked, determined to find out what she was after and be done with her.

"Great! They love me just like we knew they would."

*We* didn't know they would, Sloan thought. He'd never even been consulted.

"Only…"

*Here it comes.*

"This agent's being a real jerk,'' she said, the steel that was never far from the surface coming through in her voice. They'd been married less than a year when Sloan had discovered that his wife's heart was made of it.

"So find another agent.''

"I can't. Androse is the best…''

Sloan stared at the ceiling. He didn't want to talk to Marla. He wanted to go to bed and think about Ellie.

Then again, maybe talking to Marla another minute or two wasn't such a bad idea.

"…because I wouldn't sleep with him.'' He tuned back in to the end of Marla's tirade. Something about why she wasn't getting enough auditions.

"Why didn't you?'' She'd slept with everyone this side of Austin in the past ten years. At least, it seemed that way to Sloan.

"Sloan!'' She really sounded shocked. "You know I'm not that kind of girl.''

*Bullshit.* "Then you've changed since you left home.''

"You're right about one thing, Sloan.'' Her voice

softened, sending alarm signals through him. "The ranch is home."

Not anymore it wasn't. If it ever had been. Sloan's ranch had been a place for her to lay her head when she couldn't find anywhere better. He could have told her all of that.

"I meant Texas" was all he said.

"How are my precious babies?" she asked in the same soft tone.

Raising his arm so he could see his watch, Sloan harrumphed softly. It had only taken her five minutes to ask. "They're fine, Marla."

"Do they miss their mama?"

"No."

"Don't be nasty, Sloan, it doesn't become you." Her voice had hardened again.

But she was right. "They're babies, Marla. Their memories are short."

"Well, I miss them," she said, apparently appeased. "I've got a real nice place out here, Sloan, and I've been thinking that maybe I'll send for them."

"What?" he hollered, bolting upright.

"I'd like to have them with me."

*Think.* He forced himself to look beyond her words, to get by the image of his little demons living anywhere but at his side, tormenting him night and day. He'd die first.

"Why the sudden motherly concern?"

"I do have partial custody, Sloan, with child support rights and all."

The money. She needed money. Not the girls. Sloan felt sick. He should have fought for complete custody at the time of the divorce. He'd have won hands down.

He just hadn't seen the point of prolonging the divorce

settlement. Marla had never had a moment's interest in the girls. From the time they'd been born, she'd barely given them a glance. Unless she was on show, of course. Then she played the perfect mother.

Custody hadn't seemed important. Getting her out of his life as quickly as possible had.

"You can't ship babies off by themselves," he finally said. The case was closed.

"You'll have to bring them out to me, then."

"I can't. I'm in the middle of weaning."

"You and your damn cows. You always did love them more than you loved me."

Feeling a twinge of guilt, Sloan had to admit she was probably right. But it hadn't been for lack of trying.

"Well, I can't come there right now," she said indignantly. "I'll miss auditions."

"The twins aren't going to New York, Marla," Sloan said, standing. He was done talking to her now. "If you want to see them, you'll have to visit them here, and we both know you aren't going to do that."

After hanging up, he went in to take a shower, to scrub the memories of Marla away. The failure of their marriage hadn't been all her fault. It probably hadn't been very much her fault. He'd practically driven her to the affairs she'd had, by being unable to love her faithfully. Unable to keep his sex drive focused solely on her. He may never have had actual sex with another woman, but he'd wanted to. A lot. Almost from the beginning. Hell, from before the beginning.

And Marla had to have known.

ELLIE WAS AT WORK by six o'clock Friday morning to catch up on the stuff she should have done the night before. She was so engrossed, she didn't even notice the time pass. She'd have missed lunch altogether if her stomach hadn't been growling at her for skipping breakfast. Deciding that with a fresh mind she'd have a better chance of getting through the huge pile of work waiting for her that afternoon, she picked up her purse and headed downstairs to the day care.

She needed to eat. The girls needed to eat. Seemed logical that they eat together. Warming to the idea, she determined to take them next door to Austin Eats Diner. They'd love all the colors of the diner. And they both adored "sha-shas"—their French fries.

But first, seeing Hope Logan alone, she stopped in at the gift shop.

"How's it going?" she asked after they'd hugged hello. You'd never know at a quick glance that Hope's heart was breaking. Not unless you looked closely into those forthright blue eyes. Not unless you knew her as well as Ellie did.

Hope shrugged. "Could be better."

"Still nothing from Drake?"

"Nope." Her eyes were moist. "I'm afraid we've reached a permanent stalemate."

Ellie ached for her. "I can't believe he'd be such an idiot."

"He told me from the beginning he didn't want kids."

"Yeah, and he was young and didn't know what he was talking about."

"Apparently he did."

Ellie was afraid to ask, but afraid not to. "Has he filed for divorce?"

Hope shook her head. "I keep thinking he will."

Frowning, Ellie watched as Hope dusted off the counter by the register. "It's a good sign, don't you think, that he hasn't."

She sure hoped so.

"I don't know what to think about people anymore. Look at little Cody." Hope stopped dusting. "What kind of woman could possibly dump a newborn baby on a doorstep and walk away without looking back?"

Ellie had wondered the same thing a million times over the past few weeks. Every night when she crept into the baby's room to whisper good-night and tell him she loved him.

"Life's ironic, you know?" Hope swallowed, tears welling in her eyes again.

"How so?"

"I can't be happy without a baby, and I'm married to a man who refuses to give me one. And here's a woman who apparently couldn't be happy with one, so she threw him away."

Life was ironic. And Ellie couldn't help thinking about all the people, most of whom she loved dearly, who were being hurt by Cody's abandonment.

The woman who had done this to all of them had better have a damn good explanation.

THE GIRLS WERE DELIGHTED with their outing, and it was just what Ellie had needed, too. She felt a real rush of pleasure as she sat at a table along the wall in the colorful, unpretentious diner, a high chair on either side of her. There was just enough room between the girls to keep them from reaching each other—or the food on each other's tray.

"Sha-sha," Ariel demanded.

"Not until you take a bite of your hot dog," Ellie told her. She'd cut a hot dog up into tiny pieces and divided them between the girls, then done the same with the peach she'd ordered.

Knowing better than to argue, Ariel picked up a piece of the hot dog and put it, along with most of her fist, into her mouth.

Alisha dropped her cup on the floor. Thankful that she'd thought to bring their baby cups, with lids, from the day care, Ellie bent to pick up the drink. And was rewarded with a piece of peach on the back of her neck.

"That was a sly one, girl," she said, putting the offending piece of fruit on a napkin on the table. She took another bit off her plate and placed it on Alisha's tray. "But it didn't work. You still have to eat it."

"Sha-sha," Ariel demanded again.

"Please." Ellie smiled as she gave her one. Ariel couldn't count yet. She'd eaten at least three bites of hot dog to earn her prize. Now if Ellie could only get her to eat her peaches.

"Looks like you've got your hands full."

Recognizing the grinning young woman, Ellie smiled. "Sara! I was wondering where you were."

"I was on break."

"So how's it going?" The other woman's cheeks still looked far too hollow.

Sara shrugged, her uniform hanging on her shoulders. "Good, I guess."

Ellie didn't have the heart to ask her if she'd remembered anything. The lost look in Sara's eyes was enough to tell her she hadn't.

"You're still happy at Mrs. Parker's?"

"Very." Sara smiled, but her lips faltered when Ariel reached for her pencil with a very greasy, chubby hand.

"Ariel, no!" Ellie said, wiping off the pencil before she gave it back.

"Oh, no, that's okay," Sara said. "She was just curious."

Without looking at the baby again, Sara hurried away. But not before Ellie had seen the pain in her eyes.

## CHAPTER ELEVEN

HE'D HAD THE DREAM AGAIN. If wanting Ellie didn't kill him, dreaming about it was going to. Sitting alone in his favorite greasy spoon, Sloan frowned into his beer.

"Hey, mister, you look like you could use some cheering up."

He recognized that voice. "Roberta!" he greeted the woman, perhaps too enthusiastically, but she didn't look as if she minded.

"Can I sit down?"

"Sure!" He pulled out the chair next to him. "Have a seat. How've you been?"

He hadn't seen Roberta Lathrop in over a year. She'd been on the rodeo circuit with him years ago, and they'd kept in touch. She'd married one of his cowboy buddies.

"How's Tom?"

She grimaced. "We're divorced."

"Oh, God, Roberta, I'm sorry."

"Don't be." She smiled and, shook her head. "He's been more in love with his bottle this past year than he ever was with me. It was actually a relief to have him gone."

"Have you eaten?" Sloan asked. "I'd love to buy you lunch."

Her smile grew into something Sloan recognized.

"I'd like that, thanks," she replied.

She was a very pretty woman, Sloan acknowledged while he watched her order a tuna sandwich and potato salad. She'd been a barrel jumper, and her body was as lean now as it had ever been, but rounded where it should be. Sloan was a breast man. And a waist man. And a butt man. Hell, he was a man who liked all of a woman's body.

Lunch lasted almost two hours, and he and Roberta were both laughing so much their sides hurt as they remembered dumb things they'd done as teenagers riding rodeo. Roberta had come from a broken home, as well, and had been looking for an escape in the rodeo circuit.

She'd spent the last two hours coming on to him.

"Look—" she laid her fingers on his arm "—if you want, we could go back to my place," she offered, long after their plates had been cleared away and their beer mugs were empty. "It's just inside the city limits."

She'd been out in the country all morning at the stable where she boarded her horses—the only thing she hadn't had to give up in her quest to get out of her marriage.

"I'd love to," Sloan said. Lord knew, he needed the sex. And Roberta had been one of the women he'd been attracted to while he was married to Marla. "But it's late and I've got to get my daughters from day care before it closes."

"Another time, then."

Sloan couldn't tell whether she believed him or not. He took her new phone number and put it in his wallet. He just might need it.

ELLIE WORKED LATE Friday night, reviewing the week's events. Besides overseeing the clinic's day-to-day operations, she was largely responsible for coordinating the twenty-fifth anniversary gala scheduled for March and already had several folders full of lists and prices.

She'd been so busy she'd barely been able to say hello to Sloan when he came in to pick up the girls, and she was impatient with Connor when he interrupted her just after Sloan left. It wasn't that she didn't want to spend time with him—she did. But he seemed to have no sense of the business world all. He didn't clue in when someone was too preoccupied to just stop and chat for half an hour about nothing more than how much he was enjoying his new condo.

But even after he'd left to see if Beth would go to dinner with him, Ellie had trouble concentrating. Maybe it hadn't been Connor at all—maybe the problem was *her*. She was impatient with Connor because he was free to leave.

Ellie wanted to be that free. She wanted to be at the ranch.

The Cassidys would be having dinner, and Sloan's would be getting cold as he fobbed off whatever tidbits his babies tried to share with him while at the same time ensuring that they got enough in their bellies to keep them healthy. She wondered what they were having and hoped, for Sloan's sake, it was macaroni and cheese. The girls absolutely loved it. It was easy to chew, and didn't hurt much when they threw it.

Sloan was really going to have to work on that throwing food thing—

"What's got you so deep in thought?"

Hearing her mother's voice, Ellie jumped, surprised and embarrassed to see that Megan was standing right in front of her. She hadn't heard her come in. Glancing down at the mound of work before her, she felt a little guilty, too. She'd had no business wasting time with silly daydreams.

"Sloan and his girls." There was no point in prevaricating. Megan would figure it out, anyway. Besides, if this continued, there might very well be a problem with Ellie's work. Megan deserved to know about that.

Taking a seat, Megan crossed one leg elegantly over the other, her arms draped over the arms of the chair. "What about them?"

Ellie tilted her head. "Nothing in particular. Just wondering what they were having for dinner."

"Wishing you were with them?"

She shouldn't have been surprised, but she was. "How'd you know?"

"I know you. I also know that you've spent far too long with your nose to the grindstone, and it's time you started to live a little."

"I live." Ironically enough, her mother's words hurt. It didn't seem to matter that she'd been thinking something similar herself.

"Tell me this," Megan said, her blue eyes kind. "What suffered here the nights you went out to the ranch?"

"Nothing," Ellie quickly assured her. "I came in early in the morning and took a shorter lunch when necessary to make up for the time away. Even the day I left early, everything got done."

"And that's the point."

Ellie frowned. She wasn't following Megan.

"It's possible to work hard and have a life, too. I always have."

Looking at her still-beautiful at sixty-two mother, Ellie knew that in Megan's case, having both was possible. Beth, too, had always been able to handle her responsibilities and have fun. But Ellie wasn't like them. If she didn't stay focused, her work was going to suffer.

Besides, she thought as she waved off Megan's offer to have Harold, their butler, bring her some dinner from home, her mother and Beth weren't on trial.

Megan left, but passed Ellie's office a few minutes later on her way home for the evening.

"Mom?"

"Yes, Ellie." Megan's pure white hair, still elegantly styled after a full day's work, shone under the hall light.

"Have you heard anything back on your investigation of Connor?"

"No," Megan replied. "You'll be the first to know when I do."

"You are having him investigated, aren't you?" Ellie hated to ask, but she had to be sure. She was scared to death that at some point her mother was going to be seriously hurt by that man.

"Yes, Ellie, I am."


ARIEL WANTED ICE CREAM. It didn't matter that she'd just wolfed down her Saturday morning pancakes and bananas. It didn't matter that Sloan had work to do.

The authorities were investigating Sloan's missing cattle, the fences were fixed, and he had a full weekend ahead of him catching up on paperwork.

And two daughters to entertain. Transforming the floor of his office into a nursery was no small feat; covering the floor with quilts and carting in every toy the twins owned took an hour. But he figured the effort would buy him twice that.

Before he let the girls loose on the quilts, he stood in

the doorway, one child in each arm. "Okay, here's the deal. Daddy has to work today, you understand?"

Both babies nodded, the bobbing of their heads not at all in unison.

"Great. Now, what I propose is that if you let Daddy finish what he has to do without crying, then I will take you both into town for ice cream afterward."

"I-keem!" Ariel shouted.

"That's right." Sloan smiled. And then, very seriously, he said, "Now, do we have a deal? Daddy works, you don't cry—and then ice cream."

"I-keem!" Ariel and Alisha squealed together.

They squirmed to get down, and as one surprisingly powerful little foot caught Sloan's fly, he almost gave in to them. Almost.

Needing to let out a squeal of his own, he stood his ground, instead. "Not until I have a deal," he said. "Do we all agree? You promise not to cry?"

Ariel nodded vigorously. Sloan put her down. Seeing her sister on the floor, going for toys she wanted, Alisha nodded, too.

Free at last, Sloan reached for his crotch and groaned in pain.

And ten minutes after he started work, Ariel wanted ice cream.

"No," he told her, barely looking up from his papers. "Not until Daddy's done, like we agreed."

Not very many minutes passed before he heard from her again. He ignored the demand.

A while later, on the telephone with an irrigation man and trying to determine the least expensive way to get through the year's predicted drought, Sloan was suddenly interrupted.

*"I-keem!"* Ariel hollered. *"I-keem! I-keem!"*

*"I-keem!"* Alisha joined in.

According to his watch, he'd been working for half an hour. And he didn't have any ice cream.

Alisha started to cry. She crawled over to him, and her pudgy hands sank into his jeans as she pulled herself up.

Postponing the remainder of his conversation until Monday, Sloan stomped to the kitchen, got a tub of imitation whipped topping out of the freezer and dished up two big bowls of the light fluff. Then he added the girls' high chairs to the clutter in his office, strapped them in and went back to work.

For a few minutes. Until they wanted down again.

UP EARLY AGAIN Sunday morning, Sloan had the nursery returned to its usual location before the girls woke up. He fed them before dressing them, to avoid any clothing struggles before breakfast. And he waited until it was a decent enough hour to call Ellie.

He came right to the point. "Can you take the day off?"

"I don't know, I haven't thought about it," Ellie said, obviously just waking up. Perhaps the hour hadn't been decent enough.

He watched the girls as they ripped up a cattleman's magazine near his bed. "Okay, have you thought about it now?"

"No. Maybe. I guess I can." Ellie chuckled. "What's up?"

"I have to do the outing thing today—San Antonio this month—and I want you to come with us."

"Who says you have to?"

"It's scheduled."

"Where?" She laughed again.

He was kind of glad he was amusing her. Maybe. "I take my girls on one enrichment outing a month." He sighed. "Last month's outing was the disastrous trip to the zoo. That was the night I decided once and for all to beg for your help."

"Oh!" There was still laughter in her voice. "I must have missed that part. I don't remember any begging."

"Be still, woman, I'm trying to answer your question."

"Yes, sir."

It was a damn good thing she was half an hour's drive from him and not there in his bedroom, he thought. He'd have had to kiss the smirk he knew she was wearing right off those lips.

"Anyway, so that I won't forget, or for any other reason put off the visits, I schedule them a year at a time."

"What if it's raining?"

"We go anyway. They're a priority, and if I put them off, they won't happen."

"I can appreciate that."

There was a note of respect in her voice. He'd had a feeling she'd understand. Ellie liked goals as much as he did. His own goals had seen him through the lean years as he struggled to bring his father's bankrupt ranch back to life.

"Today's trip is San Antonio, the Alamo and River walk."

"San Antonio's an hour and a half away."

"Which is why I'm calling early," he said, hoping the explanation would serve as an apology, as well. "The girls will sleep on the way. They always sleep in their car seats, so they'll be rested when we get there."

"Okay."

"Okay?" He'd never even gotten as far as hoping that she could actually come. He'd just needed, suddenly, to invite her.

"Sure, but what about strollers?" she asked. "There are some pretty narrow places on River Walk. I don't think the double one will fit."

He loved the way she was always so practical. He'd never had anyone watching out for him before.

"I have backpacks." He hardly took the stroller anywhere.

"Give me half an hour to shower, and I'll be out."

And so he spent the day wandering through San Antonio's River District with his girls. He'd never had such a satisfying day in his life. With Ariel strapped to his back and Alisha strapped to his front, he did all the tourist things: toured the Alamo, walked along the famous River Walk, ate in one of the restaurants there, shopped a bit. All things he'd done many times before. But never with Ellie.

And that made all the difference.

THE GIRLS WOKE UP as Sloan pulled off the expressway back in Austin. Alisha recognized the golden arches off to one side of the exit ramp.

"Sha-sha!" she cried out.

"No French fries," Sloan said, slowing to a stop at the light next to the girl's favorite restaurant.

"Sha-sha!" Alisha demanded a second time.

"You've already had dinner," Sloan told her.

Ellie's glance bounced back and forth between father and daughter. What a great day they'd all had. *She'd* had. One of the best. The thought scared her to death.

"Sha-sha!" Alisha's voice was louder. She had the

finger of one hand hanging out of her mouth, but the other hand was pointing kind of haphazardly toward her sha-sha mecca. Ariel sat beside her, quietly for once, sucking her thumb.

"I'm sorry, sweetie, Daddy said no." Sloan stood his ground.

There was a loud smack as Ariel pulled her thumb from her mouth. "Cwy, Isha, cwy."

The words were said so seriously, so matter of factly that Sloan sat nonplussed in his seat. Ellie just stared. And then started to laugh. She knew she shouldn't; it was against all the rules, but she couldn't help herself. She did, however, do her best to hide her mirth from the girls.

"I can't believe she said that!" she finally managed. And when Sloan grimaced, Ellie grew serious. "Your challenge is more than just that of a single father raising twins, Sloan. They're precocious twins, to boot."

The light turned green, and Sloan passed right by the restaurant. Alisha started to cry.

"And apparently, I'm one pathetic father," he said. "She's a baby and she's got me all figured out." His jaw was tense, his lips tight.

"Lighten up, Sloan," Ellie teased. "Even you can't become perfect overnight."

He glanced over at her and grinned. "She is pretty smart, huh?"

"You bet she is."

Ellie only hoped she could follow the baby's example and be smart herself.

THE GIRLS WERE IN BED Tuesday night, the dinner dishes rinsed and in the dishwasher. Ellie had driven out after class to have a late dinner at the ranch. Charlie had outdone himself with chicken enchiladas that made Sloan want another helping in spite of the fact that he was stuffed.

"Charlie's got a girlfriend," he told Ellie as he walked her to the door to say good-night.

"You're kidding!"

Since Charlie only came during the day and usually not on weekends, Ellie hadn't met Sloan's housekeeper yet, but Sloan had told her enough about the old man for her to appreciate the particular humor in the situation.

Sloan grinned, thinking of the whistling he'd been hearing in the kitchen all week. "He met her at some rodeo over the summer and started calling her. I guess it's progressed to actual dinner dates now."

"Good for him!"

Ellie sure was beautiful when she smiled—

The phone interrupted that particular train of thought before it could get Sloan into any trouble.

He answered, but a moment later wished he hadn't.

"No, Marla, I'm not planning a trip to New York anytime soon," he said, weary of his ex-wife. She'd been draining him dry, emotionally, since she was sixteen.

Seeing Ellie standing there, watching the happy light leave her eyes as she heard who was on the other end of the line, Sloan wanted to hang up. But because he knew he was partly at fault for Marla's unhappiness, her insecurities, he tried, once again, to be patient with her.

"I'm sure there's more than one good agent in a city the size of New York," he told her. He wasn't buying the agent story. If all the man needed was a roll in the hay to get Marla work, she'd be a star already.

Ellie turned her back to him, reached for her coat, sent a wave in his general direction and walked out.

Sloan was glad. She'd saved him from making the second-biggest mistake of his life by kissing her sense-less until she decided not to go home, after all. The first biggest had been when he'd kissed her the first time, ten years ago.

He spoke with Marla for another five minutes and then, reiterating, perhaps a bit too aggressively, that he wasn't allowing the twins to go to New York whether she came and got them or not, he hung up.

And put a call in to Larry Kinkaid, his attorney, leaving a message for Larry to call him as soon as he got in in the morning. He knew Marla didn't really want those girls. She might love them in her own way—if she was capable of real love, that was—but she had actually been relieved to leave them and no longer play the "good mother" role. But if Marla had decided now that the twins were a good way to get money out of Sloan, she might just press her custody advantage. He was going to sue for full custody before she had the chance.

Marla's call had depressed him, but he was still thankful she'd phoned. The call had served him well, reminding him that he absolutely could not look to Ellie for his sexual release, no matter how many times he dreamed of doing so.

Sloan would rather die than do to Ellie what his father had done to his mother; what Sloan had done to his own wife. He'd taken Marla's innocence to appease his own appetite. And later, he'd done her wrong again each time he'd made love to her, often with someone else in mind. She'd had other lovers during their marriage, but he'd made a promise to himself not to have sex with anyone but Marla as long as she was his wife.

Taking Marla's innocence so selfishly when he hadn't loved her had only proven to Sloan what he'd already known about himself. He was a womanizer just like his father.

If he and Ellie ever got together, she would never take other lovers. But he couldn't guarantee that he wouldn't want other women himself, even just in his mind. And he would never do that to a woman like Ellie. She deserved so much more.

## CHAPTER TWELVE

ELLIE WANTED TO DIE.

She couldn't believe a human being could feel so miserable. And the tears just kept on coming.

Exchanging her soaked pillow for a dry one, she took a hard assessment of her life and the decisions she'd made.

She was a woman who looked at life realistically, accepted who she was—and wasn't. She'd met the truth head-on, set goals based on her strengths, allowed for her weaknesses.

She felt like hell. Ten years might have passed since the last time she'd heard Sloan speaking with Marla, but nothing had changed. She was still the boring, serious minded, unsexy fool who burned to make love with Sloan Cassidy.

The fool who'd actually thought, during the past week, that someday it might even happen, that maybe Sloan was going to kiss her. And more.

Unrequited longing was bad enough, but this time Ellie had traveled farther on the road to hell; she'd taken a path from which there was no return. She'd been untrue to herself. She'd promised herself that she wouldn't fall for Sloan this time, that she wouldn't even consider a romantic relationship with him. And she'd fallen for him, anyway.

Rolling over, Ellie held her pillow to her belly and

stared at the ceiling, her tears rolling unchecked down her cheeks, over her ears. She was at the ready-to-beg stage.

And she made herself sick.

Bottom line was, if she couldn't count on herself, who could she count on?

The ceiling was textured with swirls, half arcs all going nowhere, none complete. That made Ellie cry, too.

Because it was all so hard. She had goals. And she tried. And she didn't want to be pathetic. And she didn't know how to help herself—

"Hey, baby, what's wrong?"

Quickly pulling the pillow up over her eyes, Ellie turned away before Beth got a good look at her.

"El?"

She felt the bed depress as her twin sat down.

"I'm fine." The words were muffled, but would do the trick. She hoped.

"Ellie, look at me," Beth said, pulling at Ellie's shoulder. "You're lying on your bed in your suit. You haven't even taken off your shoes. Something's wrong."

"I'm just tired."

"Look at me and tell me that."

She couldn't do that. But strangely enough, she couldn't talk to Beth, either.

"It's just been a long day."

"All your days are long ones. You can come up with something better than that."

Beth wasn't going to go away. And Ellie was too beat up to fabricate any more lies. She rolled over, looked up at her twin. "I don't know what's wrong," she said. It wasn't really a lie, but it wasn't quite the truth, either.

"Something made you cry."

"I guess." She stared at the ceiling once more, taking comfort from the pillow she held. It was soft. Warm.

"Was it Sloan?" Beth asked, her voice sharpening. "I figured it was just a matter of time before he hurt you again, the slime."

"Sloan didn't do anything," Ellie said slowly, wondering why Beth's words hurt so much.

"You're sure?" Beth asked, scrutinizing her.

Staring at her sister, Ellie nodded. And then had to look away. She'd just had an awful thought. One that, once born, refused to be ignored.

"I'm not leaving here until you tell me what's got you so upset," Beth said. "You're scaring me, El."

The words left Ellie's mouth before she could think about them anymore. "I'm jealous of you."

"What?" Beth exclaimed, eyes wide. "You've got to be kidding."

But she wasn't. The truth was suddenly, sickeningly clear. "I'm jealous of you," Ellie whispered, staring at the sister she adored. Tears poured down her face, and she couldn't make them stop. She, the practical one, didn't have any idea at all what to do.

"You're so much fun to be around," Ellie said through her tears.

"Oh, baby." Beth pulled Ellie up into her arms, rocking back and forth while she cradled her. "Don't cry."

"You're so beautiful. And loving. And kind. Everyone loves you."

"They love you, too," Beth consoled.

"Men love you."

Beth was silent then, but she continued to hold Ellie, to love her. Ellie loved her sister, too. So much. Memories of the years growing up with Beth ran through her mind, both the good times and the hurtful ones that she'd always buried. The proms Beth had gone to that Ellie hadn't. The dates. The boyfriends. The cheerleading. The sorority. The fun.

"Is this why you've been avoiding me?"

A denial was on the tip of Ellie's tongue, but she couldn't make it come out. Was Beth right? With all the deep honesty she'd been indulging in, she had to really think about that one. And to acknowledge that she probably had been avoiding her sister. At least socially. She was not proud of herself.

"I guess," she finally admitted. Her heart was beating overtime, racing ahead with all of the frightening truths she was discovering. Beth didn't seem to condemn her, but Ellie was waiting for it all to sink in.

"I've always been jealous of you." Beth's words fell into the silence.

Shocked, Ellie pulled away, staring at her twin. She needed to laugh, but she was too drained. "Of me? You can't be!"

"I am."

"Of what?" She felt disoriented, trying to make sense of a life she didn't understand anymore.

"Your studiousness, for one."

"When you don't date, you find you have a lot of time on your hands."

"It's not just the time." Beth shook her head and grabbed Ellie's other pillow. "It's the focus. It helped you in school, and it helps you now. You get so many things done, you're intimidating. I never had a hope of keeping up."

Ellie shook her head. "I can't believe this."

"It's like you're indomitable, just like Mom."

Ellie was like her mother? Beth had it all wrong.

"You're the one like Mom," she said, able to set the

record straight on that, at least. "You're both so full of life, so compelling that everyone pays attention to you and ignores everybody else." Once she'd started, she found, she couldn't stop. "And you're beautiful, too. You walk into a room, and everything stops. People watch, take notice."

Smoothing a hand tenderly along Ellie's face, Beth asked, "El, you and I are identical twins."

"Tell that to the rest of the world."

Beth dropped her hand. "If you're so self-conscious of your looks, why do you wear such dowdy clothes?" she asked hesitantly. "The only difference between the way you look and the way I look is how we dress up what the good Lord gave us."

Ellie knew it was far more than the clothes they wore, that Beth would command attention in sackcloth.

Still, she was intrigued. "You really think so?" she asked.

"I know so. Take a curling iron to your hair, and you'll be a different woman."

"So why didn't you say something before?"

"I tried, but you were always so defensive of your right to be who you wanted to be."

Beth was right. Ellie *had* been adamant about holding on to her identity. At the time, it had felt as if it was all she had. She might not have liked her skin, but she was comfortable in it.

"Will you help me?" she whispered.

Beth straightened, grinning. "How soon can we start?"


CONNOR KNOCKED on Ellie's open door the next day. At least he was learning. And maybe she'd learn, too, to keep her door shut.

"Wow!" he said when she looked up. "I'd heard there was a new you! You look great!"

She couldn't help but warm under his appreciation. She'd received the same reaction all morning. It was a heady feeling. Her only disappointment had been missing Sloan when he'd brought the girls in. She'd been in the rest room. He'd been in a hurry.

"Thank you," she told Connor, standing so he could get the full effect. She and Beth were going to go shopping, but in the meantime, she'd borrowed one of her sister's tailored suits to wear to work that morning. The skirt and jacket were shorter and more fashionably styled than her usual fare. She had on Beth's shoes, too. And her makeup. The hair was her own—Beth had just curled it for her.

"I brought you some lunch. Do you have time to eat?" Connor asked, coming farther into the room when she didn't bark at him to leave.

She didn't really, but how could she refuse? She'd been looking for an opportunity to spend time with him, to get to know him better.

"Sure, have a seat," she said, gesturing toward the couch and coffee table across the room.

He'd brought chicken sandwiches and fruit from Austin Eats. He'd even gotten the drink right: diet cola. Of course, whoever waited on him at the diner would have been responsible for that.

The food was great. The company—well, Ellie was trying. Connor wasn't much of a conversationalist.

"This was so sweet of you to do," she said, smiling at him as he chomped on his sandwich. One thing was for sure, her aunt Clarise had not been as much of a stickler for manners as Megan.

"It's nothing," he said. "I was curious to see how you

looked, and you're always so busy, I figured the only way I wouldn't bug you was if I brought lunch, since you have to eat, anyway."

Okay. So all he'd been was curious—at least, he was truthful.

"You made just the right choice," she tried again. "This is delicious."

"I just told them to pack up two of whatever you usually have."

"Oh."

They chewed in silence.

"So, Mom tells me she's been showing you around Austin."

"Yeah, it's nice."

"Mom's great, isn't she?" Ellie asked, trying to put herself in his shoes. The man had just met his birth mother and couldn't tell anyone about it. How lonely that must be.

"Yeah. She's a real nice lady."

*Nice lady?* That was as warm as he could get? "I'll bet it's weird finding out all of a sudden that you have a mother you didn't even know existed."

"Yeah."

"Are you glad you found her?" *Do you have any feelings at all?*

"Yeah."

Ellie could have predicted the answer. And pulled her hair out, too, if Beth hadn't spent so much time on it that morning.

Connor was still finishing off his last bite when he left her office. She had to remind him to take his trash.

He was on his way to see Beth. When he told her that, he showed more life than he had during the entire fifteen minutes they'd spent together.

But Ellie could understand that. She'd thought she and Connor would have a special rapport since they were the only two siblings who knew the truth about his parentage. But it was Beth he was more drawn to, in spite of Ellie's makeover.

Even someone as unemotional as Connor O'Hara found Beth irresistible.

SLOAN WAS STUCK. Marla might not be the most intelligent woman in the world, but she had that steely inner core that made up for anything she lacked in intellect. And at the moment, she was desperate. It was a lethal combination.

"I told you last night, I am not sending those babies to you, Marla," he repeated for what seemed like the hundredth time. His attorney was already working on getting him full custody of Ariel and Alisha. He figured it would be pretty much an open-and-shut case, considering Marla's desertion and subsequent lack of interest in the babies.

There were only two small glitches, neither of which particularly concerned Sloan. The first was all the red tape and paper pushing, which meant things couldn't move as quickly as Sloan would've liked. The second was Marla herself. She would have the right to come and testify. And she was a damn good actress.

"I called my lawyer this morning, Sloan, and he says you don't have any right to keep them from me."

Sloan's stomach knotted. She'd already pulled out her big guns, too. He might not have the time Larry had said he needed. "You're the one who left the state, Marla," he shot back, hoping, whether he was right or not, to at least stall her. "That means if you want to see them, you have to come here."

And she wouldn't. *Please, God, let her get a job, even a small one, so she'll stay where she belongs. Away from my precious rebels.*

"That's one *option*," she said, drawing the word out. "One that, believe it or not, I'm prepared to take if I have to."

*Damn.* This wasn't his day.

The girls had been particularly challenging that morning, and he'd been late for an appointment with Larry when he'd dropped them at the day care. He'd looked for Ellie, anyway, needing to connect with her after not having told her goodbye the night before. He wanted to tell her about the custody battle he was going to be waging with Marla, but she'd been out of her office. He hadn't even seen her.

"It all depends on how badly you don't want me there," Marla continued, having let the silence draw out just long enough to be effective.

"What's that supposed to mean?" He had a pile of work in front of him and only another hour before he had to leave to pick up the twins.

"I'm your wife, Sloan." The words were almost whispered, her tone low, sultry.

"Ex-wife."

"I gave you the best years of my life. I gave you my innocence."

And she'd never let him forget, either.

Massaging his aching temple, Sloan got up from his desk and started to pace. "Get to the point, Marla."

"You owe me."

She was still the little-girl whiner he'd known back in high school. "I paid you."

"It's gone."

"That's not my fault."

"It's up to you," she said, all traces of vulnerability gone. "You get me enough money to stay here, or I have to come home. And if I come there, I'm taking the girls for my allotted time. Either way, you're going to help me, Sloan."

She knew him too well. Knew that she could count on his conscience to make him do what she wanted. Knew that he'd go to any lengths to protect the daughters he adored.

"How much do you need?" He had a couple of thousand put away—the beginnings of college funds.

She stated a sum.

Sloan slumped down so hard in his chair that it tilted backward. He could hardly believe she'd dared ask. "Thirty-thousand dollars!"

"New York's an expensive city," she said, justifying the sum herself.

He didn't have that much money to give her.

"DINNER'S IN THE FRIDGE, I'm goin'—you look like hell," Charlie said, standing in the doorway of Sloan's office.

"I feel like hell."

"Get yourself a woman," the old man advised. "Works every time."

"It's a woman that's the problem," Sloan told the old goat. Actually two women. The one he didn't want. And the one he couldn't have.

"Always is," Charlie nodded, his knurled old face looking wise. "So's it serious or just passing?"

"I'm not sure," Sloan said, needing to talk, but not sure Charlie was the one to talk to. The man pulled a hard punch, and Sloan was already down for the count.

"I need to come up with some money, fast."

The old man frowned. "You do something stupid with the books?"

"No." Sloan was too concerned over his real problem to take offense. "Either I send a chunk to Marla, or she's coming to get the girls."

Charlie's craggy face lost its color. It was the only change in his expression. "Can she do that?"

"Apparently, at the moment. She just can't take them out of the state." He hoped.

"She don't want them babies."

"Of course not. Which was why I thought the priority was getting the divorce over and getting her out of our lives, and so didn't prolong the process with a custody battle. She's got partial custody."

"What kind of dumb fool would have allowed something like that?"

Yep, he could count on Charlie to get right to the heart of the matter. "The whole thing would have drawn out forever if I'd put in for full custody, and she'd have been like a constant bad taste in our mouths," Sloan said.

"Why would she prolong it? She wanted that huge settlement you gave her as quick as she could have it. Them girls wasn't worth fighting for."

"It wasn't the girls she'd have been fighting for," Sloan told him. "It was her own damn reputation. You know Marla, Charlie. She'd never have given up complete custody—it would've made her look bad. Like she didn't love her own daughters."

"Which she didn't," the old man growled. "But you're right, she wouldn't have gone for that."

Charlie had been around to witness Marla's quick about-faces with the girls whenever someone else was around. Her sudden motherly love had been not only sickening, but confusing to the girls. More than once after they'd had company over to visit and Marla had played her part, one of the twins had crawled over to Marla later, only to be pushed away.

"I could have forced the issue," Sloan said now, the bitter taste of memories leaving him feeling sick. "But then I'd have humiliated her by having her proven an unfit mother. She would never have forgiven that. She'd have made my life and the girls' hell. And it wasn't like I was worried she was ever going to want them…"

With his silence, Charlie conceded that perhaps Sloan hadn't been so dumb, after all. Both men, with dejected faces, considered the situation for a long moment.

Charlie finally broke the silence. "You're going to have to go back to the rodeo."

Opening his mouth to ask who the fool was now, Sloan shut it without speaking. He stared at Charlie. He was too old to be roughing his body up that way. Too old to be taking those risks.

"You may be right, old man," he said, thinking hard about Charlie's suggestion. He might be too old for those risks, but the risks he faced if he didn't come up with that money were far greater.

ELLIE DIDN'T SEE Sloan the next morning, either. Still a little too fragile to test herself with him, she was out of the office when he came to the clinic to deliver and pick up the girls. Her visit with Connor had proven once and for all that no matter how she looked, she was ultimately forgettable little Ellie.

So, okay, she was fine with that. Or she was working on being fine with that. But her changed appearance *was* garnering quite a bit of attention, and she had to be prepared that Sloan would react to it, as well.

She had to be certain that if Sloan liked the way she looked, she didn't read more into it than just that, and get herself hurt all over again. She couldn't change the person she was inside. Her goal was to accept that and find a way to be happy. Sloan was attracted to the Marlas of the world. Women with pizzazz.

Maybe she could ask for some for Christmas. Did Santa deliver such a thing?

At the very least, Sloan would want a woman who didn't act as childishly as she had by running out with that silly little wave the other night.

In her office as usual on Thursday afternoon, she almost didn't answer when the telephone rang. She'd put out three fires already that day and wasn't sure she wanted to tackle another.

What she wanted was to see Sloan. He'd be there to get the girls in about forty-five minutes.

She and Beth had gone shopping, just the two of them, the night before. And Ellie was wearing her very own chic kelly-green suit. The skirt, shorter than anything she'd ever worn before, was inches above her knees. The waist-length jacket molded the figure she was used to hiding.

They'd had her hair styled and curled, too. Ellie had had to stop and stare at herself each time she'd been to the rest room that day.

The telephone continued to peal. Frowning at the offensive black object, Ellie considered letting her answering machine get the call.

She picked up instead. "Ellie Maitland."

"My entire house is filled with the mouth-watering aroma of award-winning lasagna."

"What award did it win?"

Just because she'd been hankering to speak with Sloan all day didn't mean her heart had to flip-flop just at the sound of his voice. What if, when he saw the new her, he didn't react at all?

She'd die, that's what.

"I don't know, something at a rodeo fair once. Come eat with me?"

Ellie chuckled at his desperate tone. "Be honest, mister, you're just looking for a free ride from the city to the ranch for your daughters."

"Honestly?" Sloan asked, suddenly serious. "What I'm looking for is a chance to talk with my good friend. I've been talking to myself until I'm blue in the face, but I'm not as good a listener as you are."

With one little compliment, he made her feel better than she had since she'd heard that it was his ex-wife on the line the other night. "You got more problems at the ranch?"

"You might say that. Will you come?"

"Of course."

## CHAPTER THIRTEEN

THE TWO-DAY DROUGHT from not seeing Ellie had hit
Sloan worse than the year's unusually low rainfall was
threatening to do. He was showered, dressed in fresh
jeans and blue corduroy shirt and waiting on the porch
when her Mercedes pulled into the lane. He went down,
intending to help her collect the girls out of the back,
when he was hit with a disappointment far more crushing than it should have been, considering Ellie was no
more than just a friend.

"Where's Ellie?" he asked, hoping her twin didn't
hear the regret in his voice. If he'd known Beth was
going to make the trip out, he'd have gone in to get the
girls himself. He hadn't needed a delivery service. He'd
needed Ellie.

"E-wee!" Alisha screeched from the backseat, holding her arms out toward Beth.

Ignoring his daughter, the woman stood, staring
at him, instead. Her eyes were big and brown—and
vulnerable.

"Ellie?" Sloan could barely get the word out. He
couldn't breathe. Couldn't do anything but fight the
instant hardness in his jeans, and try to stay standing.
"What have you done?"

He hadn't meant it to sound that way, but damn, was
she trying to kill him?

Looking crestfallen, she turned to pick up Alisha.

"Da-ee!" Ariel reminded him that he had responsibilities.

Reaching in for his demanding mite, he came face
to face with Ellie—the new Ellie.

"You look incredible." Sloan was embarrassed by
the hoarseness in his voice, but could not stop staring
at her. His eyes locked with hers. They could have been
completely alone for all the attention they paid to the
toddlers straining to be released from captivity.

"Da-ee! Da-ee!" Ariel wasn't going to wait any
longer.

"Okay, punkin', gotcha," Sloan said, dazed. He freed
his daughter from the restraints and hauled her up and
out of the car, all the while working furiously to come
up with a plan of action.

Okay, so Ellie had quit hiding her beauty. It was no
big deal. He'd known it was there all along. His dreams
were evidence of that. Nothing had changed.

Except that she looked so incredible in that suit, he
wasn't sure how he was going to keep his hands off
her.

But he would. Somehow he would. There was simply
no other option.

"You were right, this lasagna's delicious."

Yes, and if she continued to slide the fork over her
lips that way, he was going to have to excuse himself.

"Charlie's trying to impress his lady friend with all
his best recipes. He always takes a little of what he
makes here home for his own supper."

Ellie smiled. Nodded. He needed to run his hands
through her hair in the worst way. Just to feel those sassy
curls slide between his fingers.

No, he needed to get a grip before he ruined the best

thing that had ever happened to him. And damaged Ellie's sweet spirit in the process.

"That TV reporter has been hounding us all week," she said. She fed herself a forkful of tossed salad.

Sloan's mouth watered.

"She thinks I'm holding out on her, that I really know who fathered Cody."

"Do you know?" *Concentrate man. Pay attention to the relationship that matters.*

Ellie shook her head. "I wish I did." She laid down her fork. "Thing is, in my heart, I don't think it's any of my brothers. I know them—or at least all of them except for Connor, and I think he's too dumb to be as convincing as he is if he really were Cody's father."

"Okay." Sloan grinned.

"But at the same time, it could be any of them." She lifted her fingers. Her nails were polished. They'd never been polished before. He'd never even noticed her nails before.

"R.J.—" she put down one finger "—is the most suspicious-acting, but he's far too responsible to let something like this happen. And Mitch…" She ticked off another finger. "He didn't knowingly father Cody, but I have to believe, in all of his research, he's used some of his own sperm. It could have been stolen. This might be some big scheme to get Maitland money."

She still had three fingers up, and Sloan was slowly falling prey to her. Those damn fingers were going to play a starring role in his next dream. He was certain of it.

"Connor's already out—" another finger went down "—which leaves Jake."

"My money's on him," Sloan said, wondering why everyone didn't see how obvious a choice that was.

The man abandoned the family all the time—why not a baby?

"It's not Jake." Ellie seemed more positive about that than about any of the others. "I know he seems the most likely candidate, but it's not him."

"How can you be so sure?"

She shrugged sheepishly. "It sounds stupid, but I just know it's not. I know Jake. He'd never lose control to the point where he'd cause an unplanned pregnancy."

Ellie admired that about him, Sloan could tell.

Which left little doubt what she'd think about a man like Sloan who had to fight every minute of his life to *keep* a little control.


"WHAT WAS IT you wanted to talk to me about?" Ellie asked later, carrying dishes over to the sink, where Sloan was rinsing them. She had to tell herself not to get caught up in the domestic feelings that were taunting her.

He'd liked the way she looked, but she hadn't bowled him over. If anything, he'd been more unaware of her as a woman than ever.

Yet, for one brief second there, he'd thought she was Beth! That might possibly have been the nicest compliment anyone had ever given her. It didn't matter that he'd done it unknowingly. Or that he hadn't seemed particularly pleased when he'd realized it was just plain old Ellie, all dressed up.

For a second, she'd had his full, unadulterated masculine interest.

He put the last fork in the dishwasher. "Marla's threatening to take the girls."

"What?" All other thoughts fled as horror swamped her. "She can't do that!"

One look at Sloan's face told her otherwise. "Can

she?'' she whispered. Sloan might belong to the Marlas of the world, but Ellie felt as if those precious babies were *hers* now.

By the time Sloan finished explaining the whole sordid mess to her, Ellie wished she hadn't eaten. She felt sick to her stomach. "So how much time does Larry think it's going to take?'' she asked, falling back on practicalities. It was the only way she knew how to deal with crises.

"He's not sure, but I don't expect it'll be more than a week or two before Marla shows up here, which isn't going to be long enough. And once she's had the girls for a while, that makes my case harder to win.''

"Forget the case, she might hurt them! Or worse.'' She could tell by the look on his face that the thought was not a new one to Sloan. "So we'll buy her off,'' Ellie said as they moved into the living room. She took a seat on the couch.

Following her, Sloan settled on the opposite end of the couch, his leg flung up and hanging off the edge, just inches from her knee. Quirking his eyebrow, he said, "We?''

Ellie nodded. The solution was obvious. "How much do we need?'' She could have a money order drawn up first thing in the morning.

"She wants thirty-thousand dollars. I don't have that kind of money—not liquid,'' Sloan told her. His eyes warned her not to go any farther.

"I do.''

"I'm not taking your money, Ellie.''

His brown eyes looked like granite. She knew she had to tread carefully, but all Ellie could think about was the babies, and Sloan, in trouble. "Don't be ridiculous,'' she told him, perhaps a little more strongly than she should have. It was just that important. "I have more money than I know what to do with. What good is it if I can't help a friend in need?"

A muscle in his jaw was twitching, but it was the only movement from his side of the couch.

"The only way I ever allowed myself to seek your friendship," he began, each word an obvious struggle, "was to promise myself that no matter who else benefited from the Maitland fortune, I never would."

Sharp pains of fear shot through her stomach. "This isn't you, Sloan, it's Ariel and Alisha."

"I'll get the money."

He wasn't backing down. He'd made himself a promise. If she'd learned nothing else about Sloan all those years ago, and again more recently, it was that he kept his promises.

"How?" she whispered. Her mind was working furiously, trying to find a way to make money available to him without it's being a gift.

"There are some rodeos coming up in the next couple of weeks. I can make late entries. The purses, if I win them all, are enough to cover everything I need. And before I give it to Marla, I'm going to insist on having full custodial rights."

"Rodeos, Sloan?" Cold, suddenly, Ellie thought of the little she knew about the famous cowboy sport. "It's so dangerous."

"I've been competing most of my life."

"But you trained then. You haven't trained this time."

He looked away, his foot bobbing up and down slowly beside her knee. "The rodeo is merely a commercialized view of what cowboys do everyday, Ellie," he said. "I've been roping calves all month long. The only difference this time will be the spectators."

"What if you get hurt?" She couldn't keep the fear out of her voice. Or the fact that she cared. A lot.

"I won't."

"What if you do?"

He was looking at her, intently. She was afraid he was reading between the lines and seeing far, far too much.

"I could get hurt every single day I leave this house to work the ranch, El, or drive my truck, or even take a shower. You can't live life being afraid of getting hurt."

His voice had lowered to a timbre she'd never heard before. Somehow they weren't just talking about the rodeo anymore.

"You can if you've been hurt so bad you'd thought you were going to die."

Eyes narrowed, Sloan looked suddenly fierce. "Who ever hurt you that badly?" he asked. "Some guy you met in college?"

Ellie shook her head, praying that the tears gathering in her eyes wouldn't fall.

"It was you." Her words were no more than a whisper, sticking in her throat.

He straightened, stared at her hard. "But…"

"Because you didn't want me." Ellie had no idea why she was humiliating herself this way. She only knew it felt good to finally be able to talk about that time in her life. To get it out. Get it over.

"I wanted you." His voice was so strong, so sure.

And Ellie shook her head. "No, you didn't, Sloan, and lying about it only makes it worse. It's okay, I'm a big girl now. And I learned not to play with fire."

"I wanted you." His voice shook.

Ellie meant to blurt out another denial. Her gaze connected with Sloan's, instead. Stayed there. She pretended she saw things she couldn't possibly be seeing, so when he slid along the couch, she met him halfway. When he took her into his arms, pulled her up against him, she went willingly.

Settling her bottom on his lap, he pushed up against her. "See how much I want you?" he whispered. "How much I've always wanted you?"

Heart beating so fast she could hardly breathe, Ellie felt his arousal and was lost. Sloan was holding her, his body nudging hers intimately. It was worth dying for.

His head lowered so slowly, Ellie had time to savor the precious seconds, to anticipate the touch of his lips. His mouth settled on hers, opened hers, and she gave to him everything he asked for. Gave eagerly. Greedily.

In no way had she anticipated this. In all her dreams of Sloan, there'd never been such fire. His lips consumed hers, and she arched against him, trying to get closer still. Rubbing herself against his arousal, she gave a brief thought to her virginity, to the fact that he might not be satisfied with her innocence, that she might disappoint him. The ideas traveled slowly through her awareness and then were gone again—lost in the sharp flickers of desire Sloan was sending coursing through her.

He could have it all. The future be damned.

DELICIOUS ENERY RAGED through Sloan, sending him so far from home that he was almost lost. Ellie moaned. A sweet, needy, beautiful sound that ripped through him. He recognized that sound. She'd made it ten years ago when he'd kissed her.

And suddenly, Sloan was filled with the same

sickening sense of failure he'd known as a teenager with Ellie in his arms. He was disgusting and dirty and soiling something that, in Ellie, would be pure and priceless.

Pulling his lips from hers took every ounce of effort he had left.

"No," he panted. "We can't do this."

Jumping up from the couch, he put as much distance between them as he could. Glancing back over his shoulder, seeing her half lying there, lips swollen, eyes clouded, he was tempted to run outside, to dunk his head in the icy cold water of the horse's trough. But he was afraid she'd be gone when he got back.

And this time, she deserved an explanation. He'd never meant to hurt her. Not ever. To save her from pain was exactly why he'd stopped their lovemaking ten years before. Why he had to stop now. He just hadn't been man enough last time to tell her that.

Leaving her, apparently, to assume he hadn't wanted her. That possibility had never, ever entered his head.

How could she not know how insanely much he had wanted her?

## CHAPTER FOURTEEN

TORMENTED BY MEMORIES from the past, Ellie couldn't get up. She was cold, trembling. Beyond humiliation. Her only thought was survival. Hanging on. Getting out.

Usually so in control, at least outwardly, Sloan paced in front of the windows. Ellie wished he'd climb through one of them and be gone.

"I swore that would never happen," he said, his voice rough, angry. He seemed to be speaking more to himself than to her.

Ellie couldn't reply. Finding strength from somewhere, she slid her legs to the floor and planted her feet, preparing to stand, to make it to the door and beyond. She wasn't confident that her wobbly knees would carry her, but she had to try. She had to get away from him. To be as alone physically as she was emotionally.

"Don't go." He'd turned and was facing her again, his brown gaze pointed. Imploring. "I need to talk to you."

Ellie sank back into the couch, her foolish heart soaring even then. He needed her there. It wasn't over.

Still shaking, she waited silently while he sat beside her, turned to look at her. She withstood that look, but mostly because she had no other choice. She was suspended between life as she'd known it and life as it was to become. Whether better or worse, it was never going to be the same again. She wasn't a young girl anymore, wasn't a silly teenager with shallow feelings.

"Sex was never meant to be a part of our relationship." Sloan spoke slowly, as though choosing his words very carefully.

Ellie's heart dropped. She wasn't ready to hear this. Wasn't strong enough to make it through his rejection a second time in her life.

Yet, immobile with misery, she didn't move.

"It can't be a part of our relationship."

She yearned for tears, for any relief at all. Instead, she remained as she was, while her heart slowly died inside her. Her only compensation was that it couldn't get any worse.

"Say something, Ellie."

She tried, because he asked it of her. But her mouth didn't even move.

"You were the one who stipulated, from the very beginning," he continued gently, "that this relationship we embarked on would have to be nonsexual."

She had said that. She'd even wanted to mean it. Damn him for making her fall in love with him again.

Trying to smile, Ellie wondered if a person could freeze to death alive. If she sat here long enough, shutting down, would her heart just eventually stop beating?

"And I agree it has to stay that way." He rubbed his hands together, concentrating on them.

Ellie wished she could see his eyes, to know, once and for all, that the man felt nothing for her. He sent such damn mixed messages, they were killing her. He was gentle and warm, needing her. Wanting her. She was still tingling where the hardness of his arousal had pressed against her.

But his desire hadn't lasted past the first kiss.

"I just need you to know that it's not you, Ellie." He glanced over at her, his head still lowered slightly. "The problem is all mine."

For a kiss-off line, it was weak. Cliché. She'd expected better from him. She had to go now. Right now.

Her legs wouldn't move. Except for the trembling.

"I still can't believe you actually thought, ten years ago, that I didn't want you." He grabbed her hand.

Ellie wanted it back.

"And I can't take a chance that you'd think that now. I want you, Ellie," he said, looking so intently into her eyes that she almost believed him. "A lot."

Staring down at their clasped hands, Ellie could almost believe him.

But Sloan Cassidy didn't want Ellie Maitland.

Or maybe he did. He said he did. She'd felt his desire only moments ago. Maybe he really did.

But then why…

She glanced up, and her eyes must have conveyed more of what she was thinking than she realized.

Sloan dropped her hand, left the couch altogether. "I wouldn't be faithful to you, Ellie." The words were almost a whisper. And Ellie felt, physically, the impact of them. Her skin was cold, as though a whisper of wind had passed by her, through her.

She wasn't woman enough to hold him, she thought. After one kiss, he was that sure.

Somehow Ellie made it to the door. Stumbling down the porch steps, she had no idea if Sloan was behind her. She didn't care.

She lost a pump on the way to her car, but didn't stop for it. Dumping out her purse, she found her keys and then pushed everything back inside the bag Beth had talked her into buying. She had liked it earlier in the day.

The door handle on her Mercedes didn't work. The key wouldn't turn. Then she remembered the keyless entry and pushed the button on her key ring to unlock the door. Except that she still had to push on the handle to open it. And her thumb didn't seem to be strong enough. Using both hands, pushing on the knob with her knuckles, she finally got it to work.

When she reached the point where she was sure she was going to pass out, she fell into the car. She got the door closed, though not tightly.

She couldn't breathe. Couldn't think. And suddenly, she couldn't see, either. Not well enough to get the key into the ignition. Her eyes were blurred with tears. Big, gulping, ugly-sounding sobs were rent from her chest, filling the car's interior.

Her arms were too weak to hold on to the steering wheel, her fingers too limp to turn the key once she finally managed to get it into the ignition. She could no longer deny what she'd known for years. Sitting out in the middle of nowhere on a ranch she wanted to leave, surrounded by nothing but darkness and fear, she saw so clearly.

It wasn't the clothes that mattered. Which was why she'd never bothered with them before. It wasn't the hard work, or the goals. All that mattered was who you were. And she'd finally faced exactly who she was, who she always would be.

Ellie Maitland, loving daughter and sister, good friend to all—lover of no one.

Only problem was, Ellie didn't want to be that person anymore.

HE WAS AN ASS. An absolute jerk. Still hating himself after a nearly sleepless night, Sloan pulled slowly into the clinic the next morning. The girls were sleeping in their car seats. Little Alisha's swirled tuft in the middle of her forehead was wet with sweat where the sun had shone in through the back window. Ariel, with her perfect curls, was still emitting the occasional hiccup, left over from the sobbing tantrum she'd had after breakfast.

She'd refused to eat her bananas in her high chair. Sloan had refused to let her have them out of her high chair. Neither of them had won. She'd missed the treat. He'd had to let her go without eating the fruit she needed for a balanced diet.

Waking the girls wasn't fun. While both of them were anxious to get inside and play, neither one of them wanted him to leave.

But he'd had to. He had to get to Ellie. To assure himself that she was okay. That they were okay. Or at least salvageable.

What a damn jerk he was. Last night had brought home to him just how serious his weakness was. He couldn't even control his libido around Ellie, when it mattered most.

She was engrossed in something on her computer. Sloan stood in her open office doorway, watching her. Wishing things could be different. That his sexual desires weren't a legacy from his no-good father.

God, she was beautiful. Dressed in a purple sweater over a colorful silk blouse, Ellie shone. He wanted to haul her up on her desk and finish what he'd started the night before.

"Hi," he said instead.

Her head jerked around. She didn't look pleased to see him. As a matter of fact, her gaze was so dead,

Sloan looked over his shoulder to see if someone else had come up behind him.

No one was there.

"I'm sorry." He didn't think for a second that the words were going to excuse him—he just didn't know what else to say. And he was sorry. Sorrier than he'd ever been in his life.

"There's no need to apologize."

Her voice wasn't quite as cold, as detached as her eyes. But almost.

"Yes, there is." He came into the room and started to shut the door, but when she frowned, he changed his mind. "I behaved like a selfish bastard, and I am sorry. You're the last person in the world I'd ever want to be that way with."

If anything, his words seemed to chill her even more.

Focusing on her computer screen, she said, "Don't worry about it, Sloan. It's already forgotten."

"Then why won't you look at me?"

She did. And her eyes were empty.

"Please, can't we talk about it?" he asked. Afraid he'd lost something vital forever, that he'd killed the best thing that had ever happened in his sorry life, Sloan started to panic.

"There's nothing to talk about. It's done. No big deal."

He tried for another five minutes to get her to yell at him, rip him from limb to limb, acknowledge that something had changed, but she didn't budge. He'd never seen someone build such solid walls in such a short time.

"We're still friends, Sloan," she finally said, her voice weary. "Let it go."

And with that, he had to be satisfied. There was absolutely nothing he could do, nothing he could say, that was going to move her. At least he still had her friend-ship. Such as it was.

But whatever it was, he thought as he took the stairs two at a time back down to his truck, it was better than nothing.

SLOAN DROVE BACK TOWARD the ranch, his mind filled with nothing but Ellie. Of what he'd had—and what he'd lost. The way she'd looked right through him that morn-ing made him ache inside, to the point that he felt he couldn't get right back up and go on. He ached not only for what he'd lost, but for her—for what he'd done to her. His careless sexual advances had stolen something from Ellie, left her less than she had been. And he was never going to forgive himself for that.

He loved her, he realized while driving on the de-serted open road that led home. He loved Ellie Maitland. It had nothing to do with sex. And everything to do with the person that she was.

"Damn!" He couldn't believe it had taken him so long to figure it out. "I love her."

The knowledge left a bitter sting. It had been hard enough before to know that he could never have her, that he wasn't husband material for a woman like Ellie. Harder still knowing that she was the one woman in the world he'd ever loved.

One thing was for sure, he thought, swerving his truck into the gravel on the shoulder of the road to turn it around. He wasn't going to let what had happened the night before happen again. He was going to get serious about tending to his libido. He wasn't ever going to take it out on Ellie again.

As luck would have it, Roberta Lathrop was home when Sloan showed up at her place. She'd called out to

the ranch once since Sloan had run into her. He'd promised to look her up sometime when he was in town. He
just hadn't planned to do it so soon.

"Sloan!" she greeted him with a welcoming grin.

Sloan couldn't help but feel the difference in her
greeting compared to Ellie's earlier one. He just wished
he felt happier about it.

"You aren't working today?" she asked, showing
him into a pleasantly decorated but small apartment.
Everything was in earth tones, good quality, comfortable looking.

He shrugged, feeling out of place in her little living
room. He dwarfed the entire apartment. "I decided
to play hooky and wondered if you wanted to come
along."

"Sure!"

Her broad grin should have done wonders for his
ego.

"Where're we going? Should I change?"

She was wearing blue jeans that couldn't get any
tighter and a cotton top that outlined her breasts
enticingly.

"You look beautiful," he told her honestly.

"So where're we going?" she asked again, still standing there smiling at him.

"I don't care." He hadn't even thought about it. "The
girls are in day care, and I'm free until I pick them up
this evening."

He wondered if she'd be offended if he just came
out and asked to have sex with her. Somehow he didn't
think she would be. Roberta knew the score. And she
wouldn't care.

She'd offered to bed him even when she'd been married to his friend. Sloan would have taken her up on her

offer too, if he hadn't still been married to Marla and bound by the promises he'd made to himself the day he'd said "I do." Nor had he been willing to doublecross his buddy. He'd gone out and gotten himself tanked, instead.

Then he'd gone home and had sex with his wife.

"Come here," he said, his eyes lowering as he pulled her up against him, remembering.

"Sure!" She didn't even pretend to resist.

Sloan bent his head, kissed her, willed his body to fill and harden until it ached with need. He remembered how he'd felt all those years ago, how bad the wanting had been.

But he was still too bruised from the night before. He couldn't forgive himself so easily. He was going to have to spend a little time with Roberta. Let the anticipation build again.

Ending the kiss slowly, he smiled. "Let's go riding." He pictured her on the back of a horse, her hair flying behind her, her tight bottom moving up and down in the saddle. A woman on a horse had always been a turn-on. "We could pack a lunch and eat out someplace."

"A picnic?" Roberta played with one of the buttons on his shirt. "I'd love that, Sloan. Why don't we take a couple of my horses? They're closer to town, and that would give us more time."

"Sounds good."

And to his relief. It really did.

AS IT TURNED OUT, Roberta had sandwich makings and fruit right there in the apartment, and in no time they had a backpack filled with drinks and food, and had strapped a blanket to the back of the gelding Sloan had chosen to ride. They were off, wind in their hair, the

October air fresh against their skin as they flew across the vast open Texas plains.

Riding always settled Sloan. Put him in sync with himself. Today was no different. As soon as his butt settled in the saddle, he knew he was going to be okay. It wasn't as if loving Ellie was a new thing. The only thing new was the knowledge that he loved her. It didn't change his actual feelings any. Or what he could or couldn't do with them.

He had Roberta with him. A full afternoon planned. And by nightfall, he'd be empty of all the fire that had been eating him to the point of insanity these last few weeks. He wasn't sure why he'd been denying himself.

Purposely letting Roberta get ahead of him, Sloan hung back behind her and watched her fanny ride the saddle. Her slim waist only made her bottom more delectable to watch—and Sloan watched, all the way out to a creek Roberta knew about, nearly a mile's ride from the stable where she boarded her horses.

And if his mind wandered some during the ride, replaying the last twenty-four hours, that had to be expected. Of course, he'd think of Ellie often. She was his best friend. Hell, he'd just discovered he loved her.

He was doing this for her.

So why, after he and Roberta had eaten, when she leaned over to lick the apple juice off his lips, did he feel a stab of guilt? Why wasn't he jumping Roberta's bones and satisfying the demon inside him?

Because he was out of practice.

Rolling her beneath him, Sloan gave himself free rein, allowing himself to give in to his base instincts and have his way with a woman, no strings attached, for the first time in his life. Roberta's breasts were thick and glorious, pressing against his chest. Her lips, tasting of salt and apple juice, were full, womanly, eager.

He took them, murmuring words of appreciation. Words that, strangely enough, he had to work hard to come up with.

And while his body cooperated to some extent, he couldn't find the fire that would take him over the edge. It took everything he had to keep his mind off Ellie.

He looked into Roberta's eyes…and saw the death that had been in Ellie's that morning.

"Touch me," she whimpered, pulling his hand up to her breast.

He was touching her. But there was no magic there.

"Harder," Roberta demanded, moving her pelvis against him.

Sloan was going to have to disappoint her. Lying on the ground with Roberta, he discovered something about himself. Something that was so monumental, so life-altering that he actually started to shake, to know fear like he'd never known it before.

He couldn't possibly be getting it right. He had to be losing his mind.

And yet, as he pulled away from Roberta and sat up, his arms on his knees, his eyes focused out across the prairie, Sloan was filled with certainty.

Yes, he had a healthy libido. But he had a healthy heart, as well. And more, a healthy sense of self-worth.

"I just realized something," he told the woman who was rustling around on the blanket around him, collecting the leftovers from their picnic.

He glanced at her over his shoulder, expecting her to be angry. Her brows were drawn slightly, her downturned mouth revealing her disappointment. But her eyes, when they met his, were filled with understanding.

"Sloan Cassidy can't make love to a woman, no matter how lovely, when he's in love with someone else," he told her, still amazed at the discovery. It didn't set at all with the opinion he had of himself.

"Who didn't know that?" Roberta asked wryly. "You're the most honorable cowboy I've ever met."

Dazed, as though this were all some weird dream from which he'd awaken any moment, Sloan shook his head. "I didn't know it."

Stunned, Roberta sat back on the blanket, her mouth open. "You were faithful to that bitch you were married to until the day she left," she finally said.

Sloan shook his head. Roberta was being such a good sport. She at least deserved the whole truth. "That night in Dallas, four years ago, when you were still married and—"

"I came on to you, and you turned me down—that's what I mean," Roberta said. She pulled her knees up to her breasts, hugging them.

"I wanted you so badly I burned for weeks."

Her eyes widened. "You did?" She was grinning.

"I did," Sloan admitted shamefully. "And it wasn't the first or last time that happened. I…thought about you when I was with Marla."

"So you're human, after all!" She drawled out the words, her pleasure at the discovery obvious.

"I'm disgusting."

"No, Sloan," she said, turning serious. "You're human. Marla was a cold-assed bitch. But you're a healthy man, with a man's needs, and she was all you had."

Maybe. Somehow, coming from Roberta, what he'd

done didn't sound quite so disgusting. "I still did her wrong."

"Maybe." Roberta didn't falter in her honest gaze— not for a second. "But I don't think so. I think she did you wrong, using your goodness to get what she wanted, and then leaving you out in the cold while she went after other men."

"She always came back, apologized, came on to me." Sloan found himself defending Marla even now. Whether out of habit or because he truly could see her side, he wasn't sure anymore.

"And by that point, she disgusted you so much, the only way you could stand to be with her was to pretend it was all your fault."

Stunned, Sloan stared at Roberta.

"I'm flattered that I was able to do it for you," she finished softly, smiling.

"I should have fallen in love with you," Sloan said, not even sure he'd meant to say it out loud.

"Yeah." Roberta smiled sadly. "You should have." She stood, gathered up a corner of the blanket. "But you didn't."

No, he'd fallen in love with Ellie Maitland.

And Sloan had no idea what he was going to do about that.

# CHAPTER FIFTEEN

KNOWING SHE COULDN'T put off the inevitable any longer, Ellie pulled out the folder in which she'd been keeping the replies to the Maitland Maternity anniversary celebration. She wanted to stop counting after the tenth refusal, but knew that she couldn't keep avoiding the situation.

If nothing else, Megan deserved to know what was going on. Her mother had created magic more than once in the past; maybe she'd be able to come up with something to counteract the negative effect of all the recent bad publicity. Maybe she'd have an idea about how to gain back their good reputation in time to save the party.

Fifty. Out of five hundred invitations sent, fifty of them had been returned. Still numb from her encounter with Sloan the night before, Ellie hardly blinked as she recounted the refusals. There were still fifty of them.

She couldn't even raise a little fear over that fact. Just as she hadn't been able to shed a single tear that morning after Sloan left. The one thing he hadn't done last night was humiliate her with an apology. She'd been grateful that he'd spared her that.

He'd taken care of that little detail this morning, leaving her with nothing to be grateful for.

Damn him.

Megan was in her office when Ellie walked down

with the invitations. Damn again. She wouldn't have been disappointed to find Megan out for the day, to be spared having to admit that she was failing to maintain the clinic's reputation in the face of the challenge they'd been handed the month before in the form of little Cody.

She didn't bother to sugarcoat the bad news. "We're up to fifty refusals."

Megan paled. "That many?"

Picking up on her mother's distress, Ellie felt edgy. "I counted them twice," she said, handing the returns to Megan.

She fell onto the edge of the seat in front of Megan's desk. She'd expected her mother to have a plan in place, or at least to tell Ellie not to worry, to be confident that all would work out.

Instead, as Megan leafed through the refusals, her face was lined with worry. "Even the Sandersons?" she said, almost to herself.

"I think they were going to be out of town—a niece's wedding, they told me."

"Maybe." Megan continued to read the names on the returned invitations. "Or maybe they just said that's where they were going to be."

"What are we going to do?" Ellie asked. She'd also heard murmurings of client cancellations. Well-known clients—the ones who paid for the clinic to keep operating. Until now, she hadn't given the rumors credence.

"We have to find out who fathered that baby."

Ellie agreed with her mother.

"I've been hoping one of the boys would come forward," Megan said. "But it looks like we have no choice but to subject them to buccal testing."

Ellie's stomach lurched. It wasn't that the test was

particularly invasive physically—merely a swab from inside the mouth. But she hated to think of her proud, honorable brothers being put on the hot seat like that. As though their own mother didn't trust them.

"It'll probably take a while," she finally said. Because the men were related, their results would probably by too close for positive identification on the first level of tests. It could be months before they narrowed the prospects, by process of elimination, to one of them.

"And maybe in the meantime, something else will turn up," Megan said, clearly hoping that would be the case.

Ellie could just imagine the heyday Chelsea Markum would have if it took testing to prove that a Maitland was responsible for little Cody. If the man's honor alone wouldn't bring him forward.

"Have you heard anything back on Connor?" Ellie asked.

Megan shook her head. Her "Not yet" was so preoccupied, Ellie wasn't even certain her mother had heard her.

"We better hope something turns up soon," Megan said, dropping the refusals back into the manila folder.

Ellie wasn't great at hoping, but for her mother, for her job, she'd give it her best shot. Meanwhile, she'd better come up with a contingency plan for when hoping failed.

WHEN SLOAN CAME in to pick up the girls that night, he asked Ellie out to the ranch. Less then twenty-four hours before, Ellie had left there, promising herself she'd never, ever be back, but she accepted, anyway. He'd said he needed to talk to her, privately; that he'd wanted to take her out to dinner, but hadn't been able to get a sitter for the girls.

Since he'd already apologized, Ellie couldn't help but wonder what was so damn important that he had to see her right away, in private. She also wanted to prove to him that she wasn't broken, that they could still be friends, just as she'd said that morning.

Maybe she had some proving to do to herself, as well.

Besides, she had an ace now that she hadn't had before, thanks to him. She was numb. Through and through. Permanently. Seeing him that morning had confirmed that.

And she could hardly abandon the girls just because their father was a class-one jerk. Or maybe not so much a jerk as an idiot for not loving Ellie.

Sloan drove through a hamburger joint for the girls' dinner, letting them make a mess of the backseat of his truck as they fed themselves while he drove. Ellie had been following in her car, but had seen the gross state of things the second they got to the ranch. Ketchup was smeared all over both car seats, four hands, two faces, and everything else in between. Pieces of bun and discarded hamburger dressed the seats and the floor. There were no French fries to be seen, however.

The girls were dumped in the tub, scrubbed, dried, dressed, read to and tucked into bed within half an hour of their arrival home.

Sloan hadn't met Ellie's eyes once during the entire process.

Her stomach started to churn. If she hadn't known she was immune to him, she'd have had to attribute the knots in her stomach to fear. Since they couldn't be that, she wondered if she was hungry. So hungry, in fact, that she didn't feel hungry at all.

Still not looking directly at her, Sloan grabbed Ellie's hand as soon as the last blanket was tucked, and pulled her out of the twins' room and into the living room.

"I discovered something today," he said.

He sounded odd to her. She couldn't place why, didn't recognize the unfamiliar note in his voice. And she didn't want to be in that room with him, either. Some of last night's pain was left in that room. It was raining down on top of her.

"Wh-what did you discover?"

He sat on the couch. She refused to.

"I discovered that I'm a decent guy, after all."

She'd have thought he was joking, except that his eyes were dead serious.

"Congratulations."

"I'm serious."

"I know you are." She frowned. "I just can't figure out why."

"Why I'm a decent guy?"

"Why you're apparently just discovering that fact."

She paced in front of the couch where he sat, trying to get a step ahead of him, to be prepared.

"Please, come sit down." Grabbing her hand as she strode past, he tugged gently. "I need to tell you some things about my past, and it would be a whole lot easier if you were stationary."

Acknowledging his request, Ellie agreed to sit, but she tried to scoot down to the other end of the couch, away from him.

"Stationary and close," he said, retaining a hold on her hand.

She wanted to be strong enough to pull away from

him. To be angry that he was playing with her after his rejection the night before. She wanted to scream at him to quit sending mixed messages. She wanted to tell him he was killing her.

But he was Sloan. And she knew she loved him, even though she couldn't *feel* anything anymore. And she wanted to know why he didn't know just how great a guy he was.

"The first time my father was unfaithful to my mother, he cried." Sloan paused, looked down at their clasped hands. "They both did. He swore he'd never meant to hurt my mother, that the other woman meant nothing, and that, knowing how much it had hurt them both, he knew for certain he could never do such a thing again."

Hearing the emotional catch in Sloan's voice, Ellie had to work hard to make certain that her empathy didn't turn into more feeling than she could handle. She had to maintain her distance, the numbness that was keeping her sane.

"The second time, it was because he was too drunk to know what he was doing. The third and fourth times, it was the same. By the fifth time, my father was still crying, but my mother wasn't anymore."

Tears burned Ellie's eyes. Tears for him. She had no idea why he was telling her all this, but there was no doubt that the memories were painful to him.

"He cried every time after that, too."

"Why?"

"Because he really didn't want to hurt my mother, because every time he hurt her, he hurt himself." Sloan rubbed the back of her hand with his thumb. "The point is, he didn't want to do what he was doing, but when the time was ripe, when there was a willing woman and he was turned on, he just couldn't seem to help himself.''

"How sad.''

"Sick is more like it.''

There was no mistaking the bitterness in Sloan's voice. "He was weak, Sloan. That doesn't make him sick. Not in the sense you mean.''

"Maybe. Maybe not.''

His finger was doing bad things to her. She was going to have to leave soon, before she lost her ability not to care.

"So this is what you discovered today? That your father couldn't help being the man he was?''

She wasn't at her best, but even if she had been, she didn't think she'd be able to follow him on this one.

"No.'' He squeezed her hand, let go of it. "What I discovered is that I'm not my father.''

Ellie looked over at him. His mouth, only inches away, was so tempting. And so out of reach. "I don't understand,'' she admitted, embarrassed. He'd apparently expected more from her.

"From the time I hit puberty, I've loved women,'' he explained, his words tumbling out all of a sudden. "Didn't matter what shape, size, color hair, or how intelligent she was, I'd start thinking about sex and getting turned on.''

"Yeah.'' Ellie had grown up with three healthy brothers. She knew how their minds worked.

"I even dreamed about them.''

"Yeah.'' She knew about wet dreams, too, though not from her brothers. She'd learned about those in her psychology class at the university. Of course, knowing that Sloan's experiences were classic textbook material didn't stop her from feeling jealous of all those other women who'd turned him on.

"I was only fourteen years old and already just like my father."

"No!" Ellie's shocked gaze found his troubled one, and she tried to determine whether he really believed what he'd said.

"I thought I was. Even after I'd had Marla, I couldn't get my mind off other women."

"Boys are that way, Sloan," Ellie told him. "They can't help it."

"And they grow out of it."

"Yeah, most of them do. Or at least learn to control it."

"I didn't."

"You were unfaithful to Marla?" That shocked her. She'd never have believed Sloan capable of something like that.

"No."

Unnerved at how relieved that admission made her, Ellie just nodded.

"But I wanted to be."

Ellie sat quietly while Sloan told her about the ways that, in his own mind, he'd been unfaithful to Marla. He talked about the fears that had driven him through all the years of his marriage, that had made him forgive a wife who was unfaithful to him in so many ways, a wife who didn't love him.

"All along, I thought it was me—that it was my inability to love only her that had made her the way she was."

"Marla was always fooling around," Ellie said derisively.

"Not always." Sloan's voice was low. "I took her virginity when she was seventeen."

"She told you that?" Ellie scoffed. "And you believed her?"

Frowning, he nodded. "I was there, Ellie."

"Sloan, Marla slept with my older brother Jake when she was sixteen. I know this for a fact because they were caught in the act, and my parents were furious!"

Ellie, overhearing the argument from the stairs, had been furious, too. Jake had always been her hero, and she couldn't believe he'd done something so stupid—with someone so shallow.

She'd assumed Sloan had known that. And she'd never been able to understand why someone as honorable as Sloan would hang out with a woman like Marla. Except, of course, that she was fun and had a great body.

"Jake and Marla?" Eyes wide with disbelief, Sloan stared at her.

She nodded slowly, trying to gauge his reaction. She'd never have said anything if she hadn't thought he knew about Jake and Marla's relationship.

"She wasn't…she faked—" Sloan broke off.

The couch started to shake, and Ellie got really worried. Was he crying? Did he really care about Marla? Even after all this?

Ellie looked around for an escape. A way to leave her whole darn life and start over somewhere else. Someplace where she could just be Ellie whoever.

Taking a sideways peek at Sloan, she was shocked to see that he was laughing.

"I can't believe it," he said. And then added, "Yes, I can. She's one hell of an actress. I just didn't know how good she really was."

"You're not mad?" she asked tentatively.

"Hell, no! Well, maybe a little."

Ellie didn't see how he *couldn't* be mad. After all, Marla meant a lot to Sloan. He'd rejected *her* because he'd been so in love with Marla. The woman had been gorgeous, even back in high school. Later, she'd been his wife.

"I'm angry that I married her because I thought I'd taken her innocence."

"That's why you married her?" Eyes wide, Ellie couldn't help staring at him.

Sloan nodded. "It's one of the reasons."

"Oh."

"I can't believe I wasn't the first. Can't believe she lied to me!"

Ellie shouldn't be feeling this pleased that he wasn't heartbroken over her revelation. She tried not to pay any attention to her own feelings. She wanted to be numb.

"I've been feeling guilty for almost half my life for taking her virginity so callously when she was still so young." Sloan laughed without humor. "Now I find out I didn't do anything of the sort."

"It must feel good to be free from that, at least."

He sat silently for another couple of seconds, shaking his head, a bemused look on his face. "I'm going to be pissed as hell when I have a chance to really think about this," he finally said. "I'd probably never have married her. My whole life would have been different."

"Then you wouldn't have had Ariel and Alisha, either."

He stopped short. "You're right, of course."

Sloan was so close that she could feel his warmth, smell the fresh spring scent of the soap he used. His jeans were brushing up against her tight linen skirt, the dark and light blues contrasting perfectly.

But that was all that was perfect about her and Sloan. She had to get out of here, get back home where she belonged, where she remembered who she was.

"So what brought all of this on today?" she asked him.

"I'm not done with the past yet."

"Oh." What more was there?

Lifting her hand, Sloan took it between both of his, almost as though he were afraid she was going to dart out on him. Ellie's stomach tensed when he wouldn't meet her eyes.

"The reason I did what I did ten years ago—"

"Did what you did?" Ellie interrupted. She couldn't go there. Not tonight. Not after last night. "You didn't do anything."

She'd surprised him. He studied her for a couple of long seconds, and when he spoke this time, he didn't look away. "Knowing what kind of man I was, I'd promised myself from the very beginning of our friendship that I would never lay my hands on you."

Ellie forced herself not to drop her eyes, when what she wanted to do was run and hide.

"You are pure and innocent, so beautiful. You would never survive life with a man who was unfaithful to you. I couldn't take a chance on damaging something so special."

"I have no idea what you're talking about." She couldn't believe his nonsense. She just couldn't.

"That night I kissed you, Ellie, I hated myself. I'd been wanting you from the very beginning, but I'd never meant to touch you. I was sick that night, afraid that I'd never be able to leave you alone after that. And I knew that I had to quit seeing you altogether before I ruined your life."

And what he'd done *hadn't* ruined her life? He'd stolen whatever little confidence she'd had in her sexuality, in her ability to please a man. Granted, she'd had no confidence to begin with and her own shortcomings couldn't be laid at his feet, but still...

"You don't think I should have had some say in my own future?"

"You only saw the best in me, El. You'd never have believed that I'd hurt you."

Unable to reconcile what he was telling her with what she'd believed for so many years, Ellie knew she was going to have to think about things later, when she was alone. She was afraid he was saying these things because he felt sorry for her. That he was just trying to make her feel better.

"What happened last night is what prompted this, isn't it?" A dull throb started at the base of her neck.

"In a way," Sloan admitted.

Ellie tried to pull her hand free, but he held on to her.

"I lost control again last night and felt history replaying itself."

"Surely, you don't still think you're anything like your father!"

Shrugging, Sloan said, "Last night I did."

*History replaying itself.* Could all of this really be true? He looked so sincere that it made her heart ache. He'd never lied to her before. And yet...

"But today you know differently?" she asked, starting to hope in spite of the voice of self-preservation that was screaming inside her head, telling her not to be a fool a third time.

Sloan looked away from her, but he didn't drop her

hand. "I lost your friendship the last time, I wasn't going to lose it again."

It wasn't much, but Ellie exploded with happiness, anyway. Whether Sloan desired her or not, she did matter to him. He cared.

She could settle for that.

Sex wasn't everything. Hell, for Ellie, it was pretty much nothing.

"I went out this afternoon intending to have sex, get it out of my system, so that I could trust myself not to risk that friendship."

She went hot. And then cold. Taking him by surprise, she jerked her hand away. He'd called her over here to tell her he'd had sex with someone else this afternoon so he could be friends with her? And she was supposed to be glad about that?

Well, maybe that would be the logical thing to do. Ellie felt crushed.

"Am I supposed to thank you or something?" she asked when the silence grew deafening. She'd meant to be sarcastic, but the words came out sounding as pathetic as she felt.

"No." He took her hand again and turned her to face him. "Ellie, I couldn't do it."

Her gaze shot up, searching his.

"I was with a woman I've wanted on and off for years—a woman I knew on the rodeo circuit. She offered, I was right there, but I couldn't do it." He spoke quickly, his voice urgent. "What's more," he added, "I didn't *want* to do it."

"You didn't?" She was still staring at him, unmoving, except for the rapid beat of her heart.

Sloan shook his head. "I discovered that I can't make

love to one woman when I'm in love with someone else."

"Are you?" she whispered. She felt overwhelmed by her disappointment. He'd called her over to tell her he was in love with another woman. That he didn't need her help anymore.

She should be happy for him. She *had* to be happy for him. And she would be. Soon.

"I am."

His eyes glowed so much that it hurt her to look at them, so she stared down at her hands, instead. "Oh."

"That's it?" he asked, lifting her chin until he could see her eyes again. "I tell you I love you, and you say, 'Oh'?"

Adrenaline flew through her. "Me?" She could barely get the word out, could hardly breathe.

"I love you, Ellie. I don't want any other woman, just you…"

Ellie couldn't stand to listen to any more. His words were too beautiful. Too surreal. She was too starved for them to be able to take them in. And too afraid that he just didn't know his own mind. His desire probably stemmed from lack of sex. She knew in her heart that once they'd made love, he'd grow tired of her.

But knowing that didn't stop her.

Throwing herself at his chest, she silenced him without even thinking about what she was doing. She planted her lips on his and ate the words she couldn't bear to hear.

# CHAPTER SIXTEEN

SLOAN DIDN'T FIGHT HER. How could he? After ten years of wanting her, there was no longer any reason not to give in to the desire singeing his veins. And, he hoped, hers.

Surprised at the strength of her kiss, her boldness, he didn't hold back, taking of her sweetness, denying himself nothing. Her lips were soft, supple, hungry and yet untutored. With his tongue, with his mouth, Sloan taught her how to mold her lips to his, to open to him, to taste him as he was tasting her.

Heaven couldn't be any better. He'd never known a real home before, but he knew beyond doubt that he'd just found it. Right here in Ellie's arms.

Her weight was slight on top of his body. Nestling down farther in the couch, he pulled her more fully on top of him, fitting her hips over the juncture of his thighs. The pain of having her there was almost more than he could bear, and at the same time gloriously perfect.

"I never dreamed it would be like this," he said, whispering his love.

She groaned, and he thought he heard "Me, neither," but he couldn't be sure. The thought was soon lost as he was consumed by feelings he'd never experienced before.

"I have to make it good for you," he murmured.

"Tell me how." The need was urgent to make this the best night of her life, the best lovemaking she'd ever experienced.

"It's good…"

"I want to undress you," he murmured against her mouth, and then drew back to look into her eyes. He wanted her with him all the way. No doubts. For the first time in his life, the sex wasn't for him. It was all for her—the woman he loved. Whatever she wanted, whatever she needed, he had to give it to her.

She smiled shyly, then looked down. "Okay."

Touched by her bashfulness, Sloan kissed the tip of her nose, silently ordering himself to slow down. "You're sure?" he asked her. It was going to kill him to stop, but he would do it in a second if that's what she wanted.

"Yes."

There might be embarrassment in her voice, but her eyes told him everything he needed to know: stopping was going to kill her, too.

"Shall we move to my bedroom?" he whispered, not waiting for an answer before he sat up, scooped her into his arms and carried her down the hall.

Ellie ran her fingers through his hair, distracting him.

"You're sure you want to do this?" he had to ask. His bed was just ahead, unmade and ready for them.

"I've never been more sure of anything in my life."

Sloan laid her down on the bed, intending to join her immediately. But first he turned on the light and reached for the sleeve of her jacket. "Let's get this off you before we wrinkle it." He kept his words quiet, calm. As they'd entered his room her eyes had grown as frightened as a fawn's. He had no idea what had intimidated her, knew only that he had to make her feel safe again.

"It's permanent press," Ellie said. She sat up, all business as she helped him remove the jacket. And then she sat awkwardly, watching him fold it and lay it across a chair.

Sloan came back to the bed, so hard he could barely move. "You okay?"

Licking her lips, Ellie nodded.

Bending down, he took those lips in a searing kiss, wiping out thought for both of them. A hand on either side of her, he guided her back down to the pillows, exploring her mouth with his tongue—and was shocked by a spate of hot desire when her tongue joined his in the mating ritual.

With his mouth still joined to hers, Sloan went to work on the buttons of her blouse, slowly undoing each one, taking his time. Giving her time. He eased the blouse off her shoulders, breaking the kiss to watch.

Her breasts were straining against the bit of lace she was wearing for a bra. They were big and round and about the sexiest things he'd ever seen. "Lady, you are blessed."

"Sloan!" Ellie covered herself.

"No way," he protested, holding her hands above her head. "I don't know if I'll ever let you cover them again after this."

"I'd get arrested."

"Displaying art isn't a crime." His gaze jumped from her breasts to her eyes and back again.

She chuckled. "Indecent exposure is."

The sound was Sloan's undoing. Groaning, he came down on top of her, splaying her breasts against his chest.

"You, too," Ellie whispered throatily, pushing at his shirt.

Sloan ripped it off in one yank, hardly aware of the buttons spinning off around them.

He lowered himself slowly, touching his belly to hers, skin to skin, and then ribs to ribs. She was hot. And soft. And more than he could handle. Sloan's arms went weak and as he fell he rolled at the last second so he could take her on top of him.

He loved her then. Every inch of her. With his hands, his lips, his words. He had to know what she felt like everywhere, behind her ears, her neck and shoulders, her glorious breasts with nipples that peaked at his first touch. He counted her ribs, slid his fingers along her back, her sides, her bottom. And beyond.

And when she was panting, crying out for him to help her, he spread her legs.

"Yes, Sloan," she clamored breathily. "There."

He knew where. He knew how.

And when she was completely ready for him, he sheathed himself and mounted her.

Ellie, bucking up against him, didn't give him time to go slowly, to savor the touch of her body against his. She opened to him, and he was at her entrance, pushing in.

Pushing harder than he should have had to, as ready as she'd been.

"Mmm," she moaned, forcing their joining herself when Sloan held back. And when she'd done the deed, he lay still within her, holding himself up on his elbows while he watched the glazed look of pain slowly recede from her eyes.

"You should have told me." He was shocked. Elated. Angry.

"Don't be mad," Ellie whispered, her body clenching his intimately.

"I could have made it easier for you." There were several things he could have done, would have loved to have done.

"I didn't want easy," she told him, her voice surprisingly steady. "I wanted you."

The overwhelming happiness shining from her beautiful blue eyes, echoing in her voice appeased him some. "I still—"

Pulling his head down abruptly, Ellie kissed him. "Sloan!" she said firmly, turning him on all over again. "Shut up and love me. Please?"

As her voice drifted off, he did just that.

And it was a long time before either of them could speak again.

FOR THE FIRST TIME in her life, Ellie knew the hell of the morning after. And she wasn't lucky enough to be paying for just too much to drink. No, what she'd gone and done was much more invasive than a few drinks. And much harder to recover from.

Managing to avoid Beth when she'd come home sometime after midnight had been a near miracle. Missing both Beth and her mother that morning had been by design. It was Saturday, and she'd been in the office before either of them were out of bed.

She hadn't been able to face them.

She hadn't even been able to look at herself in the mirror that morning. She'd done her hair and minimal makeup by touch, avoiding any chance of meeting her own eyes. Of seeing the fear she knew was there.

But she couldn't avoid feeling the pain. The panic. Sloan had had sex with her.

There was no mystery left. She wasn't vibrant or

compelling. And it was only a matter of time before he didn't want her anymore.

At seven-thirty that morning, sitting alone in her office, Ellie turned cold with horror. She'd been thinking about Sloan again, trying to be brutally honest with herself, when suddenly—

"It's me," she said aloud, aghast. "All along it's been me." She'd spent her whole life believing that she was a disappointment to everyone around her. That she didn't add up. She'd spent twenty-five years knowing that all she really had was herself. That she was the only one who accepted her as she really was, the only one who found her worthy.

Except that, no matter how many times she replayed the night before, she couldn't convince herself that Sloan had been disappointed. It had been completely the opposite, in fact. Looking at herself through his eyes, she had to admit that her self-image was taking a radical turn. He'd made her feel so damn special that she was scared to death.

Scared to let herself be happy.

Aside from some ignorant business associates, the world didn't think Ellie Maitland was a loser. Beth, Lana, her mother, Sloan—they'd all tried to tell her that. Ellie was the only one who'd found herself unworthy. Nobody else.

And she had no idea what to do about that.

HEARING A COMMOTION out in the hall later that morning, Ellie escaped from the torment of being alone and went to investigate.

The last thing she needed was what she found.

"What in hell are you doing here?" she demanded

of the nosy TV reporter. She had no more patience for the irritants in her life.

"I have someone I want you to meet," Chelsea Markum said.

Ellie didn't trust the smile on the other woman's face. It was just too much "cat got the cream" for Ellie's comfort.

Before Ellie could turn her back on the avaricious woman, Chelsea had pulled her companion forward. "This is Tanya Lane," she said, as though the name should mean something to Ellie.

It didn't.

Not liking the hungry look of the stylishly dressed stranger, Ellie felt goose bumps slide up her spine. The woman was beautiful, in a cold sort of way. And, Ellie feared, dangerous.

"You've never heard of me, have you," the woman demanded haughtily.

"No." Ellie answered her slowly, trying desperately to size up the situation. To remember if she'd ever met the woman before. At a party, maybe? Had Ellie snubbed her without meaning to?

"Now, why doesn't that surprise me?" the other woman drawled. "Though he apparently didn't find me newsworthy enough to warrant mention to his family, R.J. did find me worth sleeping with."

"Who are you?" she demanded through gritted teeth. She was fed up, and wanted the woman out of there.

"She's R.J.'s ex-lover, just like she says," Chelsea reported happily. "And what's more, she's the mother of that little babe you all are hiding so carefully."

Never had Ellie been delivered devastating news with such glee.

Just as she thought things couldn't get any worse,

Ellie looked up to see Connor lounging against the wall behind them. By the look on his face, it was obvious that he'd heard every word. And thought the news just as distasteful as Ellie did.

The woman had to be lying.

Ellie was beyond caring why Connor was at the clinic on a Saturday. She returned to her office, slamming her door in the reporter's face. She had to call her brother. R.J. would straighten this whole thing out.

CHARLIE WAS GETTING MARRIED.

He broke the news during lunch, shortly after the twins had gone down for their afternoon nap. He'd still be living in his same house—still coming to work for Sloan—just not sleeping alone anymore.

"Congratulations, old man." Sloan broke off a piece of homemade bread and dipped it in the chili Charlie had made that morning. He was happy for Charlie. And a little worried, too.

"You might not go in for commitment yourself, but you could damn sure sound a little happier for me," Charlie grumbled.

The curmudgeon slurped the chili from his spoon. Sloan couldn't imagine a woman choosing to live with that sound for long.

"I go for commitment," he corrected, though mainly to distract Charlie from the rest of his statement. Sloan wasn't completely happy for Charlie. He was afraid the old man was going to get hurt. But he wasn't going to tell him so. He couldn't bear to burst Charlie's bubble.

"On the surface, maybe—not where it counts." Charlie slurped some more, then wiped his mouth on his sleeve.

"You're a crazy old bastard." Sloan didn't have time

for one of Charlie's slinging matches. He had paperwork to do before the girls woke up.

He had some thinking of his own to do. Like figuring out why, when Ellie had suddenly pulled back from him last night, emotionally at least, he had been relieved.

And admitting that, why was he counting the hours until he would see her again?

"Why do you think you saddled yourself with that witch, stayed with her all them years?"

"Because I'd slept with her and I wasn't going to be like my father."

Charlie swore, his rugged face scrunched with disdain. "You are just like your old man."

Feeling as though he'd been shot, Sloan jumped to his feet, clearing his half-empty bowl off the table. He'd finish his lunch in his office. Get to that paperwork.

"You don't know what you're talking about." He bit out the words on his way through the door.

"I know exactly what I'm talking about, you disrespectful imbecile," Charlie spat. "I was his best friend."

Sloan froze, bowl suspended in front of him. "My father didn't keep friends."

"S'right," Charlie said. "Which is why I *was* his friend. Back in grade school and part of high school, before he figured out that having me around was too much trouble."

Swinging around, Sloan glared at the old man. "You never told me."

"Would you have taken me on if I had?"

They both knew the answer to that one.

"I'm not like him," Sloan said. As of yesterday, he had proof.

"Sure you are. Exactly."

"My father was a womanizer. If she had the right parts, he'd take her."

"Your father was afraid of loving and losing," Charlie said, his eyes distant, softer than Sloan had ever seen them. "His mama died when he was eight. Did he ever tell you that?"

"No." His father had never had a conversation with Sloan that Sloan could remember. Certainly not about family history.

"She was trampled by a horse right here on this ranch."

Stomach churning, Sloan set his bowl back on the table.

"Your daddy was the only one home with her at the time. He watched the whole thing."

*"Damn."*

"His daddy never did get over her death, which meant that your daddy lost both of his parents that day. And I think he blamed himself."

The nerves in Sloan's jaw ticked. He knew what it felt like to grow up without parents. But at least he had never known what it was like to have them and then lose them.

"He changed after that," Charlie said, applying himself to his chili once again.

Sloan needed to sit down, yet at the same time he wanted to flee. "I'm still not like him."

Charlie dropped his spoon back into his bowl, seemingly unaware when chili splashed out onto the table. "Why do you think your old man could never keep his promises to your mom?"

Ellie's words of the day before sprang to mind. "Because he was weak."

Charlie, head shaking, jutted out his lower lip. "Nope. It was because he didn't love her."

"Sure he did!" Sloan had seen his father's tears.

"Nope," Charlie said again, his tone brooking no argument. "He wanted to, he hated that he didn't, but he never loved her. If he had, he'd have been by her side until the day she died."

Eyes sharp, Sloan stared the old man down. "Then why'd he marry her?"

"Same reason you married Marla. There was no risk."

"You're crazy."

"You can't lose if you don't love."

He was sure there was a comeback, something that would pinpoint the flaw in Charlie's logic. Sloan just couldn't come up with it at the moment.

"Why do you think you have such trouble with them girls of yours?"

"I love them." There was no way Charlie could convince him differently. Sloan had no doubt about how much those twins meant to him.

"I know you do, as much as you know how. But…"

Hands on the back of his chair, Sloan pushed it into the table, sending more of Charlie's chili out onto the table. "What in the *hell* are you talking about?"

"It's harder to discipline them than to give in," Charlie said, sitting back with his arms folded across his chest. "Making them mind takes more of an investment. More commitment to loving… Might also be a little fear there that if you take too hard a line with them, they might not love you back."

Sloan turned cold as Charlie's words washed over him. There was a ring of truth in what he said.

Could that be why last night, when Ellie had come

a second time in his arms and then pulled away from him, he'd let her go?

He loved her. He knew he did.

But could he risk committing himself body, heart and soul to her?

Could he risk the hurt? And would anything less be enough?

R.J. WAS OUT OF TOWN for the weekend, climbing a mountain someplace. Ellie was just going to have to wait to get her answers. Her reassurances. No matter what R.J. said, Chelsea was going to run her story—that was a given. The most Ellie could do now was hope that the cleanup wasn't too big a chore. Surely, when R.J. wouldn't corroborate—

"All that's left, then, is something for the opening session."

Ellie forced her thoughts back to the task before her. She was meeting with Walton Smith again. Obviously as busy as she was, he'd asked for the Saturday meeting. Plans for the maternity care convention were almost finalized, and then Ellie's part in the affair would be done.

"Would you like some more soda or coffee?" Sara interrupted them. Because she'd wanted to keep Walton away from the clinic while Chelsea was still there hanging around, Ellie had appealed to his sympathies and begged a lunch meeting. Austin Eats had been the only place there'd been time for.

"I'd like more coffee, thanks," Walton said, smiling at the young waitress.

Ellie shook her head. If she drank any more soda, she was going to overdose on caffeine. Her nerves were already strung taut.

Sara brought the coffeepot over, and as she poured, Walton asked her a little bit about herself. His concern was obviously sincere when he heard of Sara's plight.

"She hasn't remembered anything?" he asked Ellie after the waitress had left their table.

"Nothing." Ellie shook her head, uncomfortable while she watched Sara work her way around the room, unknowingly charming her customers.

Walton's gaze continued to follow Sara. "Can you imagine how afraid she must be that she'll never remember her past, never have a life to live?"

Feeling as though an arrow had stabbed right through her heart, Ellie swallowed.

"It's almost like being dead alive," he added.

Yes. It was. Staring at Sara, Ellie heard Walton put into words what it was that she had in common with the lost young woman. The fear of never having a life of her own to live.

She was nothing but a fraud, Ellie thought. She wasn't strong. She wasn't a go-getter. All her life she'd been a coward, hiding behind her goals, and her twin, because she was afraid to risk herself emotionally.

"I owe you an apology," Walton said, his gaze also following Sara.

"For what?"

"My short temper the last time I was here. I—"

"It's okay," Ellie interrupted him, not wanting to even think about that day. "I never should have left you sitting there for so long."

"Circumstances can't always be helped, young lady," Walton said. His pale brow wrinkled. "I'd like to explain my overreaction if I may."

"Certainly."

"The last time we met was the first anniversary of

my dear wife's death. I thought working would make the day easier. Instead, I managed to offend everyone I came into contact with.''

## CHAPTER SEVENTEEN

SHOCKED, FEELING IMMENSE compassion for the older man, Ellie shook her head. "You didn't offend me."

"Family is important, Ms. Maitland," he said, his glasses slipping down his nose with the force of his delivery. "The most important thing, when all is said and done. That's why I so enjoy doing business with Maitland Maternity."

"Because we're in the business of making families?" Ellie rather liked that image. She also liked the reprieve he was giving her from her own thoughts.

"Because you *are* a family."

Feeling strangely more at peace, more energized than she had all day, Ellie dared to press the older man. "So you didn't think because I was distracted by my friend's babies that I wasn't capable of doing my job?"

"Good Lord, no!"

Letting out a huge breath, one it seemed she'd been holding for months, Ellie smiled. "Boy am I glad to hear you say that."

"Never let yourself get caught up in believing that work is the only thing in life." His words were delivered sagely, almost as though in the space of minutes the man had become the grandfather she'd never known. "Not only does it make you a very dull girl, but work makes a very poor bedfellow, as well."

Her work was what made her dull?

"I found out too late that work will never be the companion to me that my Lorraine was."

"I remember after my father died," said Ellie, "my mother's loneliness was so severe at times that I was afraid it would kill her." She shivered, remembering those days and how frightened she'd been.

"But knowing Megan, I'd wager that she was also filled with a great peace for the years she'd had with William."

Walton Smith was a smart man. "I guess you're right," she told him.

"I admire and respect your mother so much," he continued. "She's really managed to do it all."

He might have the eyes of a comparative stranger, but he had twenty-twenty vision when it came to her mother.

"You remind me of her," he said.

"My sister Beth said the very same thing."

SOMETIME LATER, after another visit from Sara to clear away their sandwich plates, Ellie and Walton returned to business—the opening session of the maternity convention. The party was always huge, a memorable event for all the visiting dignitaries and their guests.

"We've got sixty thousand dollars in the budget this year," Walton told her, "but I can't think of a single thing we haven't already done in the past."

*Sixty thousand dollars.* Marla was demanding thirty thousand from Sloan. As her foot bounced beneath the table, Ellie's mind raced ahead, formulating the plan that was going to keep Sloan out of the rodeo.

If he loved her enough to accept her help.

And if not, then she had to know that. Now.

Whether she had the strength to act on any of the

discoveries she'd made about herself, to make changes, she didn't know. But one thing she was sure of was that she wasn't going to fool herself anymore. About anything.

"Let's take them to a working ranch," she said, presenting the bare bones of an idea that could turn out to be great for everyone. "We give them some real cowboy flavor, let them know they've been in Texas."

Walton nodded and smiled, listening. Considering herself lucky that he hadn't said no right out, Ellie continued to brainstorm on the spot. "We could rent a ranch for the evening. Cater every kind of cowboy food imaginable, grill the best cuts of beef. We could offer horseback rides to any who wanted them, have a real cowboy demonstrate some rodeo tricks to entertain. We could put up video screens that people could watch while they're eating, and finish up the night with a barn dance."

"Yes!" Walton seemed almost as excited as Ellie. "You're a genius! This is perfect—something different, something that will let them relax, be comfortable for a change."

"Exactly."

"You think we can do it all—rent the ranch, hire a rodeo cowboy, bring in dinner, a band, lay a dance floor, hang lights—for sixty thousand dollars?"

"I'll make up the difference," Ellie assured him. "And I already have a ranch in mind."

For which she was going to spend thirty of Walton's sixty thousand dollars. She hoped.

ELLIE DIDN'T GO BACK to the clinic after her meeting with Walton. She didn't want to run into Chelsea Markum or her patsy again until she'd had a chance to speak with R.J. The woman's vehicle was still in the parking lot when Ellie saw Walton to his car sometime after two. Chelsea and her companion, waiting for R.J., apparently hadn't believed Ellie when she'd told the two barracudas that her brother was out of reach at least until the following morning.

Climbing into her Mercedes, Ellie drove up and down the streets of the town she'd lived in all her life. Funny how she could live twenty-five years believing she was one thing, only to find that she'd been lying to herself all along. Sad, really, when you couldn't even count on yourself.

She played out several scenarios for approaching Sloan about the dude ranch party. In one she asked him, as his lover, to do this for her. In the others she took a more businesslike approach, hitting him where it really mattered. In his wallet.

Except that she didn't think his wallet mattered to him that much.

She thought about the type of guy Sloan was. Loyal, yes. Honorable, of course. Kind, certainly. Reliable, always. Sexy, hell yes. But was he a man who would put his love for someone above all else? That he cared for her, she couldn't deny anymore. But did he need her? Did Sloan really allow himself to need anyone?

Thinking back ten years, she knew he'd never really needed her then. He wouldn't have been able to walk away so completely if he had.

But one thing became very clear to her as she drove. Putting love above all else was vitally important to her. She couldn't live any other way.

Which meant that, if she was ever going to have any kind of relationship with Sloan Cassidy, she had to know where he stood.

Calling the ranch from her cell phone, Ellie reached
Sloan's housekeeper, Charlie.

"Sloan's out on the ranch," the old man reported
when he heard who was on the line.

Though she and Charlie had still not met, it was obvious the man knew who she was. Ellie cautioned herself
not to make too much of that fact.

"He got a call and sped outta here before the girls
was up from their naps. I'm just hanging around till
someone gets here to watch over them."

Taking that as an invitation to come out—the reason
for her phone call in the first place—Ellie promised to
be right there. She headed out of Austin, praying for
courage.

SLOAN STILL WASN'T at the ranch when she arrived late
in the afternoon.

"I don't know where he's got to," said an old man
who could be none other than Charlie as he greeted her
at the door.

Ariel was clinging to the man's pants, and Ellie bent
down to pick her up. "Did he say where he was going?"
she asked.

Hearing Ellie's voice, Alisha came barreling out of
the living room. "E-wee! E-wee!"

Charlie grabbed the toddler up before she could run
Ellie over. "He was rushin' out the door so fast, I just
caught somethin' about them thieves," he said as though
they hadn't been interrupted. He didn't even flinch when
Alisha stuck a slobbery finger in between his lips.

He kissed the finger and kept right on talking around
it. "I thought he was just goin' out to fix some more
fence, but he wouldn't have been this late if that's all it
was."

Ellie tried to ignore her rising concern. Surely Sloan was all right.

"Sha-sha!" Ariel said.

Looking at the weathered old man, Ellie asked, "Have they had their dinner?"

"It's in the oven. Baked macaroni."

"Sha-sha!" Alisha cried.

"Not tonight, pets." Ellie set Ariel down in the living room, and gave the little girl a stack of blocks. "Maybe his watch stopped," she suggested to Charlie as he limped in behind her and set Alisha next to her sister.

"Wouldna mattered if it did. Sloan can tell time by the sun just as easily as he can using any old watch. He never stays out past dinnertime since he had them girls."

Ellie played with the girls while Charlie got their dinner on. When it was ready, she sat right there with them, concentrating on their chatter. And when Charlie left to find someone to take a look around the ranch, Ellie bathed the girls, read to them and put them to bed. If she stole an extra long hug or two, neither seemed to notice. Or mind.

By the time Charlie called to tell her a couple of guys were out driving around Sloan's four thousand acres looking for him, every nerve in Ellie's body was shaking. Something had definitely happened to Sloan.

She paced the entire house, snooping around Sloan's office for things that told her about the man she loved. The books he read. How neat he kept his top desk drawer. His bedroom occupied a few minutes, too. But when the unmade bed caused tears to spring to her eyes, she moved on. Eventually, she ended up out in the kitchen, sitting alone at the big wooden table, staring out into the moonlit darkness beyond the window. The barn was down there. Maybe if she looked long enough, a light would come on, telling her that Sloan was home safe, stabling his mare.

She sat there another fifteen minutes, watching, willing something to happen. The barn light didn't come on. Ellie saw her life in that darkness. The emptiness that had been her constant companion.

And that was when she knew that she wasn't giving up. Sloan was going to make it back to her safely. He had to. She couldn't think anything else. And when he arrived, she was going to find out once and for all if he loved her enough to make a life with her.

She'd wasted the first part of her adulthood; she wasn't wasting any more. Life was too short, too uncertain to take chances on tomorrow. She might never get there.

And if Sloan didn't love her…

Well, she'd face that challenge when, or if, she came to it. One thing at a time. Right now she needed to expend all her thoughts on getting him home.

SLOAN RODE LIKE THE DEVIL. Charlie was going to be spitting fence posts by the time he got back to the house. The old man had a hot date with his fiancé. They were going to Austin to have supper and look at wedding invitations. And it was way past dark.

But he'd nailed the bastards who'd been stealing from him. They'd given him a hell of a chase. Coming on horseback like they had had surprised him, but it had also been their undoing. Too bad for them that the guy they were stealing from was training for the rodeo. Once he'd finally caught up to them, Sloan had had them both roped and tied before either could put up a fight.

With a performance like that, he was pretty much

guaranteed to win Marla's money. Then Ellie wouldn't think he'd been such an idiot for choosing to ride rodeo again.

Charlie's old truck wasn't in the yard when Sloan rode up. But Ellie's Mercedes was. Sloan's gut leapt in anticipation, in spite of himself. He wasn't really ready to see her yet. Wasn't quite sure where his heart stood on things. But he was damn glad she was there, anyway.

Hoping that Charlie got to keep his date—and wasn't going to rake him over hot coals Monday morning—Sloan took care of Ronnie in record time, not even bothering to flip on a light. The moon was shining so brightly that he could see all he needed to.

As he approached the house, he saw Ellie silhouetted in the kitchen window. Catching a whiff of himself, he wished he'd taken time down at the barn for a rinse, but he figured a shower for two would be a far better use of the water.

"You're back!" Ellie jumped up before he was all the way in the back door. Throwing herself in his arms, she clutched him so tightly that he could hardly breathe.

"Oh, God, Sloan, I was so afraid!"

It took him a couple of seconds to figure out that she was crying. Alarm sharpened his senses, settling in his gut, as well. Sloan held her away from him. "Afraid of what, baby? Did someone hurt you?"

Pushing her aside, he strode through the house looking for any disturbances. The only thing he found out of place was the tidiness. All of the girls' toys had been picked up and put neatly into place.

They'd only get them back out in the morning.

"I was afraid you were hurt or something," Ellie said, sounding a little calmer as she followed him down the hall toward the bedrooms. "Where were you?"

He stopped in his tracks outside the girls' bedroom door and stared at her. "You were that afraid for me?" The sensation was entirely new. No one had ever worried about Sloan before. No one. There'd never been anyone who had cared enough.

He wasn't sure he liked being responsible for someone caring that much.

"Of course I was afraid for you—you're hours late!"

Bemused, Sloan almost smiled. Except that he wasn't sure he felt like smiling, either. "I caught the cattle thieves," he said. "I thought Charlie would be here."

"He was, until he went to find someone to search the ranch for you."

"Oh."

After a quick phone call to head off the search, Sloan peeked in on his devilish daughters, sleeping snug and warm in their cribs, before heading into his bedroom. He hoped when he got there that things would make more sense. Feel more normal. That he'd know which direction to turn next.

"I got a call from a kid who lives a couple of miles from here. Said he saw some guys hanging around the fence along my south pasture. I spooked them before I got there and ended up in one hell of a long ride before I finally caught them."

"You got them yourself?"

Ellie didn't look nearly as impressed as he'd thought she would.

"I did," he confirmed, still feeling pretty damn good about it.

"You could have been killed!"

Because things were getting a little too thick for him to handle, Sloan did the only sure thing he could think of. He pulled Ellie into his arms and kissed her words away.

"I'm just fine," he whispered against her lips, and then kissed her again. She tasted so good. Better even than he remembered.

"I have to take a shower," he said the next time he came up for air. He couldn't touch her soft skin or run his fingers through her short sassy hair with grit on his hands.

"Mmm." She pulled her mouth away from his. "I'll wait."

He was all set to ask her to join him, but the look in her eyes made him stop. Ellie wasn't ready for sex. She had something deeper on her mind.

He'd known making love with her wasn't going to be taken lightly by her, or without true intent. He just hadn't thought the reckoning would come so soon.

Sloan worried about that look in Ellie's eyes throughout the longest shower he'd ever taken in his life. She needed answers.

He was afraid he didn't have any to give her.

ANY LINGERING HOPES he might have had for an easy night were crushed when Sloan came out of the shower to find Ellie waiting for him at the kitchen table. He knew how it felt to need the safety of that hard wood in between them.

"I've got some dinner heating in the oven for you," she greeted him when he entered the room wet-haired, but otherwise decent. She stroked his ego, too, the way she stared at his chest, left bare by the shirt hanging open above a clean pair of jeans.

He read the hunger in her eyes and felt a bit better. If he couldn't come up with the right words to make her happy, he knew of another way to convince her not to dump him.

Sloan joined her at the table. "Have you eaten?"

"No." Ellie nodded toward the oven. "There's enough there for two."

She rearranged the fork she'd set out on a napkin in front of her. He ran his finger around his empty plate, thinking about how beautiful she looked. Her suit was lavender today, the skirt straight and several inches above her knees. She was sleek and sexy and way too good for him.

"I have a favor to ask of you."

The words seemed to come from left field. "Shoot," he said. Favors were easy. A lot easier than feelings.

"I want to rent the ranch for an evening."

"Rent the ranch?" He stared across at her. "What for?"

"Maitland Maternity is sponsoring a convention on maternity care…"

Ellie went on to describe the evening of cowboy fun she'd like to provide to the conference dignitaries. He saw no reason for her to look so nervous about the whole thing. She didn't have to rent his ranch. He'd give it to her. For a hundred parties if she wanted it. He told her so the first chance he got.

"That's not all…"

The look was back in her eyes again.

Sloan got up to check on the macaroni in the oven. Determining it warm enough, he busied himself with removing the casserole, dishing up a couple of plates of pasta and delivering it to the table.

"I was wondering if you'd entertain them," Ellie said when he was seated again. "You know, demonstrate some rodeo stuff."

"Sure!" That was all? Maybe life with Ellie was going to be a piece of cake, after all.

"Sloan, how can you say yes when you don't even know what it pays?"

"Doesn't matter what it pays." He took another bite of pasta. "I'm happy to help you."

He'd expected his willingness to ease the tension lining Ellie's forehead. It didn't. She wasn't eating, either.

"They're going to completely take over your place, Sloan, run lights, lay a dance floor, bring in caterers. There will be production people, a band, the works."

He could stand anything for a short time. Especially for Ellie. Sloan took another bite of macaroni. He was hungry enough for both of them.

"It pays thirty thousand dollars."

He quit chewing. "Bringing in all those people costs that much?"

"That's what they're paying you for the use of your place and your talents."

Sloan dropped his fork. "You're kidding, right?" He didn't mean to stare her down, but he couldn't help himself. The exact amount of money was just too convenient.

Ellie shook her head. "Thirty thousand dollars. I can have the contract drawn up in the morning."

Getting up from the table, Sloan cleared away his plate, no longer hungry. "Who are you trying to kid, Ellie?" he asked, focusing on the dishes in the sink instead of the woman still seated at the table behind him. "You're trying to pay my way out of the rodeo."

"The offer is legitimate. I didn't make it up."

He turned, looked at her. "But you orchestrated it, didn't you."

"Yes."

He had to hand it to her, she was right up-front with him about it. "Then thanks, but no thanks."

"So you can help me, let me use your ranch, turn it into a circus for free, but I can't help you by offering to pay what I'd have to pay anyone else for the evening?" She got up from the table, leaned back against the counter by the sink, her arms crossed as she watched him.

"That's different." He wasn't proud of the answer, but it was the best he could do.

"How is it different, Sloan? Why is it different? Because one leaves you vulnerable and the other doesn't?"

Maybe. Hell, he didn't know. "Of course not."

"You told me last night that you love me. Did you mean it?"

There it was—the question he'd been dreading. It had just arrived in a more distasteful package than he'd envisioned.

"What does that have to do with the thirty thousand?" He felt himself trying to claw his way out of a hole he'd been living in his entire life.

"Everything."

Something was different about Ellie. She wasn't backing down. Or moving away. She stood her ground next to him, demanding that he do this with her. As one part of him wondered if his lovemaking had given her this confidence and gloried in the fact that she'd found it, another part of him missed the old Ellie. The one he could count on to let him off the hook.

"One has nothing to do with the other, Ellie."

Her chin jutted out a little farther. "Yes, it does. If you love me, you love all of me. That includes my money.

If we're in love, then what's mine is yours and what's yours is mine."

"Exactly." He jumped on her last words, ignoring the rest. "What's mine is yours, which means you don't pay me for the use of it."

"Then I just give you the thirty thousand dollars as a gift, and you gift me the use of the ranch."

No! That wasn't it at all. "I will not have people thinking that I'm after you for your money."

"So your pride means more to you than I do?"

"No!" Where was she coming up with this stuff? "Of course not."

"Then you'll take the money?"

And then what? How could he survive without his independence? Sloan turned to her, took hold of her arms, pulled her close enough to almost touch him. "I can't, Ellie, please try to understand."

She dropped her eyes. "You don't love me."

"Of course, I love you!"

"Then need me, Sloan." When she looked up at him, there were tears in her eyes. "Please need me," she begged, her voice trembling.

"I love you." He gave her what he could.

"Do you need me?"

"I want you."

"But do you *need* me, Sloan?"

He wanted more than anything in life to give her what she wanted. But his throat froze, and he could only look wordlessly back at her.

Nodding, Ellie wiped her eyes with the back of her hand, grabbed her purse and walked out his front door, closing it quietly behind her.

## CHAPTER EIGHTEEN

ELLIE WOKE UP to the sound of Cody crying. Either the alarm clock by her bed hadn't gone off, or she'd shut it off in her sleep. It was half an hour past the time she normally rose. And "normal" was important now.

She didn't remember why right away. She was too exhausted to form much of a coherent thought. Other than to wonder why no one was helping the baby.

The night nurse would be gone, Ellie understood that. But where was her mother—and Beth?

Stumbling down the hall in her wrinkled shorty pajamas, Ellie reached the baby just as his cries were turning from pathetic to angry. "There you go, little fella," she said, lifting him out of his crib. His weight was warm against her breast, comforting her when she hadn't known that she needed to be comforted.

But the contact brought it all back to her: Sloan's inability to give her the real thing; the long drive home: the hours she'd lain awake in her bed, more dry eyed than not; the emptiness that faced her.

Tempted to crawl back into bed with the baby cuddled up against her, Ellie figured she'd better first find out what had happened to the rest of her family. Cody wasn't dressed or fed yet.

She had to go all the way to the first floor to find any sign of life. And that was in the form of voices in the living room.

Beth was in there. And Megan. And a man. Was R.J. here? She'd missed the news the night before, the breaking of the latest scandal. Approaching the door slowly, Ellie considered sneaking back upstairs to sleep through the day.

She would have, too, if the new Ellie had let her get away with the cowardly act.

Opening the living room door, she wondered if they'd called a family meeting without her. Everyone was there—her mother, Abby, Anna, Mitch and Connor, Beth. Everyone but R.J.

"Ellie, we were just coming to get you," Megan said, smiling when she saw Ellie on the threshold. Family meetings were serious. They were for dealing with crises. They weren't for the grins that her siblings were passing back and forth among them.

"Nice duds, sis," Mitch said. He was sitting on the couch next to—

Ellie almost dropped the baby when she saw who was sitting there, in her home, next to her brother, at her family meeting.

"Good morning, Ellie. Sorry if we woke you," Sloan said.

He didn't look sorry at all.

After her sleepless night, after the way he'd broken any dreams she'd ever had, Ellie was not happy to see him. "What are you doing here?"

"Sloan called us all early this morning," Megan said.

Her mother's calm voice of reason was familiar. Safe. Ellie concentrated on that.

"He's just finished explaining a few things to all of us."

"Where's R.J.?" Ellie focused on the practical. This meeting needed to be about R.J.

"He'll be flying in sometime this morning."

"Did you ask him about—"

"When he gets here, Ellie. Another couple of hours wasn't going to make a difference. I spoke with Ms. Markum late yesterday, and she agreed to hold her story until R.J. gets here if we agree to speak with her afterward."

"We agreed?" The conversation was getting a little ludicrous, considering the situation, but it was one Ellie could sink her teeth into.

"We did," Megan nodded once, slowly. "Better that she have the facts straight, no matter what they are."

"Let me have him," Beth said, rising to take Cody from Ellie.

Ellie pulled the baby back out of her sister's reach. She wasn't ready to relinquish his warmth. His innocent, unconditional love.

Ignoring her siblings, she finally turned to Sloan. "Why did you come?"

Every pair of eyes in the room was trained on Ellie. She felt them boring into her. They almost distracted her from Sloan's slow descent to his knee in front of her. Almost, but not quite.

Cody was taken from her arms just in time for Sloan to take both of her hands in his.

"I called them because I know that everything that happens in this family of any import happens with you all together. Your decisions are made as a team—at least the ones that matter. And believe me, Ellie, this one matters. More than I'll probably ever be able to tell you."

Out of habit, Ellie looked to her mother. Smiling,

with a hint of tears in her eyes, Megan gestured back to Sloan.

"Eleanor Maitland, I love you to the depth of my soul," he said, his gaze steady. "I need you, not merely to exist, but to live. And I want to live, Ellie. So badly, I want to live."

Ellie couldn't find a single thing to say. His image, blurred by tears, was so precious to her, and seemed more dream than reality.

"Please, say that you'll marry me, babe."

"I—"

"I'm sorry it took me so long to get to this point, but it wasn't until you walked out last night that I finally understood. One day with you is worth any risk, Ellie. It's life without you that's unbearable."

"I—" Ellie's throat was so tight she couldn't speak.

"Tell him you'll marry him, already," Beth almost shouted, jumping up from her chair.

"Come on, sis, put the poor guy out of his misery." That was from Mitch.

Abby took a long sip from the coffee she held. "Put yourself out of your misery," she added.

Megan laid a hand on Ellie's back. "Now, Ellie."

Ellie burst into tears, losing control just as Sloan rose to pull her into the haven of his arms.

"It's okay, baby, I love you so much," he murmured, burying his face in her hair.

"I love you, too, Sloan, more than I can even believe."

"So you'll marry me?"

"I'm a Maitland—"

"I know."

"Y-you're okay with that?"

Sloan included her entire family in his glance. "Are we okay with that?" he asked the room at large.

"We're okay with that," everyone answered, pretty much in unison.

"What about the thirty thousand?"

"You can write me a check today. I'll overnight it to Marla just as soon as I have signed custody papers."

"You're getting married?" Beth asked, coming over to hug them both.

Sloan's eyes were only for Ellie then. "Are we?" he asked.

"Where are the girls?" she asked suddenly. If she married Sloan, she'd be their mother. Next to being his wife, she couldn't think of anything she wanted more.

"They're with Dora, dear," Megan said.

Ellie could just imagine what those urchins were doing to the Maitlands' housekeeper.

"Ellie." Anna moved into the small circle that had gathered around her sister. "If you don't say you'll marry that man, I will."

"I'll marry you," Ellie blurted. When it came right down to it, the words weren't hard to say at all.

Her family might have gathered around them. They might have cheered, patted her on the back, heaped good wishes upon her and Sloan. But if they did, Ellie didn't know it. She was completely consumed by the adoring, unbelievably happy look in Sloan's eyes.

Ellie Maitland was finally good enough.

* * * * *